CALI MANN

Found

Thornbriar Academy Book One

This book was professionally typeset on Reedsy.
Find out more at reedsy.com

Contents

1

Hailey

I squeezed my hands together, the rough bitten fingernails digging into my skin. Even with my enhanced vision, I couldn't see a thing in the all-encompassing darkness. The night passed slowly in the closet. I knew wallpapered walls surrounded me, covered in tiny roses, stained yellow and brown from legions of smokers who once called Hastings House home. Even though I could reach out and touch the peeled edges, I still felt like I was floating in endless black space.

My arms were wrapped around my legs, and I leaned my chin on my kneecaps. The closet no longer fit my seventeen-year-old body. I didn't have enough room to stretch out, even to sleep. My ears pricked at the sound of mice scratching at the wall. A furry body ran over my foot, and I grabbed it, snapping my jaws at the creature. It squeaked, and I let it go. My whole body itched as if my skin was too tight on my frame. Closet punishments were so much harder during my wolf phases.

The door creaked open, and I stared at the empty room, my eyes adjusting to the moonlight that streamed in through the thin curtains. Had three days passed already? Three days since I bit Rose's arm? She'd made the mistake of picking on Cassie, the newest and youngest addition to Hastings House.

"Out with you, girl," snapped the female warden. Her gray hair was tied back in a severe bun, and her hawk nose took up most of her face.

They never bothered to learn our names, even after I'd been a prisoner here for more than ten years. In petty revenge, I never learned theirs either.

"To bed," Hawk Nose commanded.

I stumbled out of the cramped closet, trying to get my legs under me again after being in that tiny space for days. I headed out the door and down the musty stairwell to the dormitory floor. All of us slept in one big room on steel cots with thin lumpy mattresses. Still, after the closet, even my cot sounded like heaven.

The dim hallway stretched out in front of me, as dark and dank as my life. Moving down it, I heard a giggle from the end, and I marched toward the sound. My stomach growled. There'd be no food until morning. Maybe I should take another bite out of angel-faced Rose.

Girls, ranging in age from six to seventeen, clustered around a small heating vent set in the wall. We all wore the same bleached white nightgowns like we belonged in some musical on TV. I strolled toward them as casually as I could on my sore legs. My bare feet were silent on the wood floor. It wouldn't do any of us any good to be caught out of bed after hours. I didn't want to go back to the closet anytime soon.

"They're talking about you, Hailey." Rose's lower lip jutted out, her bandaged arm hanging by her side. Her dark eyes flashed with ferocity, but it was show. They were all terrified of me.

"Oh, really?" I leaned against the wall, feigning carelessness. Tension strung along my nerves. Had Mr. Hastings found out? About my episodes? He didn't tolerate anything different, anything imperfect.

"He's gonna sell you off," Cassie squeaked, her blonde pigtails bouncing. She was six and had only been here a month or two. Cassie still called for her mommy in her sleep. She wouldn't see her, not ever again. None of us would.

I growled, the sound rough and harsh in the silent hall. A wolf night. I'd spend my dreams chasing rabbits and howling at the moon.

As one, the girls trembled and appeared ready to bolt like a herd of deer.

Shoving my black hair out of my eyes, I scowled at them. They all knew I was a freak. There was no hiding it when we all slept in the same dormitory. They'd seen all my phases. Mermaid nights when I woke drenched in seawater, crow dreams when I cawed as I soared the skies, and fire phase...well, there had been more than one near disaster on those nights.

But the girls knew better than to tell him. So, how had he found out?

With a wave of my hand, I marched forward. The girls skittered out of the way. Folding my tall frame down to crouch by the vent was harder than it had been when I was younger, but I made it work and I listened.

"She's a virgin," said the unmistakable grumbly voice of Mr. Hastings.

I shivered. The heavyset, balding man had been the one to lure seven-year-old-me into his car, telling me that he was looking for his lost puppy.

Taking a breath, I coughed at the heavy scent of pine cleaner. The floor had been scrubbed this morning. Rose had done it, and she always used too much soap.

A woman's voice said, "Eighteen and a virgin? She'll fetch a high price."

"Everyone will want to pop that cherry." Mr. Hastings chuckled.

I could almost see him rubbing his fat hands together like some cartoon villain. He rarely came upstairs, leaving our care to three female wardens, but I would never forget his appearance.

"Next month then," the woman said. "On the 30th."

"A grand auction," he said. "We'll be richer."

"And rid of a troublesome brat," she said sourly.

"Cheers to that," he said, and glasses clinked.

Closing my eyes, I shuddered. My eighteenth birthday was a month away. Unfortunately, I had lived long enough in Hastings House to know what a virgin auction was. Fear wound around my spine like a snake.

Mr. Hastings hadn't been patient enough to wait for all the girls to grow up before he sold them off. I'd comforted more than a few over the years after they returned from servicing a customer. TV portrayed the sex act as something loving and fun, but the girls had come back devastated. Their stories of pain and blood had chilled me to the bone. I shuddered. The a virgin auction was different from a one-time customer. I'd actually have to go live with whoever bought me.

Hearing a giggle, I glanced down the hall. Girls peeked around the doorway, eager to see my reaction. Schooling my features, I frowned at them, and they ducked back.

I listened again at the grate, but even my more sensitive wolf-night ears couldn't pick up any more voices. I heard the crackle of a fire and smelled burning wood from Mr. Hastings' fireplace, but nothing more.

Standing, I squared my shoulders. I had a month. I scanned up and down the dark hallway, at the barred windows on either end. Not only did I not want to be sold off and raped, but if I lived somewhere else, my secret would be exposed. They'd find out I was a freak.

Padding down to the front window, I looked at the grassy yard. Billed as a home for wayward girls, Hastings House claimed to be a Christian charity. Though it sat just off the main road that led into the town, no one came near the iron fence that encircled the overgrown grounds. Insisting on the need to keep the girls safe, Mr. Hastings employed human guards to patrol the property as well as canines. My wolf growled at the thought of the rottweilers.

Inside, the wardens kept us on a strict daily schedule of sleeping, eating, and chores. We were allowed one hour daily of recreation which most girls spent glued to the TV, seeking visions of a happier life. Any deviation was met with strict punishment: beatings, deprivation, or closet time. I'd experienced them all in my ten years here. I scratched at the scar that ran along my back from the whipping I'd received when I'd tried to escape before.

But I was younger and less experienced then. This time I'd succeed.

2

Hailey

As I scrubbed the supper dishes the next day, I considered my options. I'd spent the whole day cataloging escape routes from Hastings House. While Mr. Hastings tried to make us as self-sufficient as possible, we still lived in the modern world. The housing and care, if you could call it that, of a hundred plus girls required some planning and assistance from the outside. We had food deliveries, laundry was sent out to commercial washers, and so on.

One of the wardens came up behind me. I could smell her hydrangea perfume before she touched my arm. It stank, and I rubbed my nose with the sleeve of my dress. Spinning around, I stared at Doe Eyes. She was the youngest of the wardens, with big blue eyes and a heart-shaped face. On first glance, one might mistake her for a kind woman, but no girl ever made that mistake twice.

"You have a visitor," Doe Eyes said.

"A visitor?" I growled, my wolf getting the best of me.

She slapped me hard and sharp across my cheek, and then she curled her hand around my arm. Her long nails dug into my skin through the worn fabric of my dress sleeve.

The plate I was holding slipped from my hand and crashed against the metal sink before slipping under the water.

"Come on," she muttered, yanking me out of the kitchen and down the hall.

There wasn't any use resisting. All of the wardens were built from pure steel. Besides, I have to say I was a little curious about a visitor. Mr. Hastings wouldn't be giving me to a customer if he expected to sell my virginity, so who could this be?

Doe Eyes shoved me into the bathroom and under the shower head. Then, she turned on the faucet, and cold water poured over still-clothed me. After a minute or two, she tugged me out and sat me on a stool. She pulled a brush through my unruly hair and tore off my soaked clothing. After helping me into a short red dress, she blow dried my hair and tied it back with a red bow.

I glanced at myself in the broken mirror that ran over the counter top. I looked ridiculous, like a wild animal dressed up for tea. My dark green eyes were liquid pools in my pale face, paler after the confinement in the closet. While my black hair was bound, wisps slipped free and danced around my face.

Doe Eyes pinched my cheeks as if that would help their color, and she ran a red lipstick across my lips. Frowning, she inspected me and sighed. "That'll have to do."

Carrying a pair of red dress shoes, she pulled me out into the hall and down the stairs. At the door of Mr. Hastings' study, she shoved the shoes at me and jerked her head.

I reached down and slipped them on. The shoes were a size too small and hurt my feet. I grimaced and stared at the chestnut-colored door. None of us went inside unless we were really in trouble. Through the wood, my wolf ears picked up the murmur of male voices and I took a breath.

Neither Doe Eyes nor I moved. We stood frozen as the voices grew louder in argument. Then, Mr. Hastings caved.

"All right," he snarled. "Ten minutes. No more." The door opened. He shoved me inside, and he and Doe Eyes departed.

I blinked. The fire in the fireplace was built too high and the small space was stuffy and hot. Two large high-backed armchairs sat in front of the fireplace, their woolly green fabric set off by the red bricks. Between them stood a table on three spindly wooden legs and, on its surface, a decanter of brandy and two glasses, one empty and one full.

A man rose from one of the chairs. Taller and slimmer than Mr. Hastings, he had a full head of curly dark brown hair sprinkled with grey. He wore a well-fitted black suit, meant to leave room for his muscled arms and chest. He approached me slowly, and his nose wrinkled as if he smelled something sour.

"Do I smell bad?" I asked.

"Like flowers, hydrangeas," he muttered.

"That'll be the warden. Her perfume."

He sniffed again and nodded. "It's fading."

I arched an eyebrow, annoyed and curious at the same time. Who was this man? And why was he behaving so strangely? He paced around me, inspecting me from top to bottom. "Like what you see?" I snarled.

He met my eyes, and the intensity in his gaze made me look at the floor. Leaning close to my ear, he whispered, "Your wolf called to me."

Stiffening, I glared at him. How did he know about my wolf?

"And my wolf answered." Studying my face, he frowned. "I am here to rescue you."

I snorted. Men only wanted one thing, and it was never to save us. If I let him help, he'd expect something in return. Besides, I had my own plan to escape; what did I need him for? "I don't need to be rescued."

"Of course not." He glanced at my tawdry dress, and the corner of his lip lifted. He continued, his voice coated with sarcasm, "Hastings House- Home for Wayward Girls is exactly where you want to be."

"And what would I owe you for my rescue?"

8

"Owe me?" His dark brown eyes studied me again, then he huffed and scratched his neck. He gestured for me to sit in one of the green chairs. "I think we got off on the wrong foot."

I sat on the very edge of the cushion, and tried to discreetly push off the heels of my too tight shoes, but I kept my eyes on him.

"My name is Noah Reed." He pushed a loose curl back out of his eyes and sighed. "I'm a recruiter for Thornbriar Academy, and I wouldn't have even been in this tiny town except there's a family of bear shifters not far from here who's youngest has come of age. Mrs. Martin has a hard time letting any of the cubs go, but the baby is the hardest . . . ." He trailed off when he saw the confusion on my face.

Shifters? An academy? What was a recruiter? I didn't know what to ask when so many questions swirled through my head. Finally, I blurted, "You have a wolf?"

Dropping down onto the other chair, he said, "Yes, I'm a wolf shifter." He grinned. "As are you."

I'd watched as much TV as anyone. I knew the word, but . . . "I've never changed into a wolf."

"You wouldn't until after your eighteenth birthday. But you're having the dreams?"

I nodded. A flutter ran through my stomach. I'd been having dreams for years. Even when I could hear better and smell better after a night of chasing rabbits in my mind, I still never imagined it meant what he was suggesting. Shifters weren't real. They were just stories.

"And you feel like your skin is too tight some days or you snap at your fri—" He glanced around. "At the others here?"

"Yeah," I said, scratching my forearm where the cheap material rode up.

"Thornbriar Academy is a place for young shifters like yourself. You can learn about your powers and how to control your abilities."

A wolf shifter? Me? It didn't seem possible. And they somehow had a school? I licked my lips.

Mr. Hastings banged on the door. "Two minutes!"

"Listen," Mr. Reed said. "We don't have much time, and I need to get you out of here. Will you come with me?"

I shook my head unsteadily. There was too much to process. I needed time to think. I already had a plan, and getting locked up in some academy wasn't part of it.

"Hailey, isn't it? Surely you don't want to stay here." His lip curled in disgust. "You know what he plans to do with you."

"I do," I said. But I would find a way out. I hadn't gone to school since I was a kid. I'd be just as much a freak at Mr. Reed's school as I was here. I squeezed my hands in my lap. "I can't go with you."

Mr. Reed frowned, but he slipped a card from his pocket and pressed it into my hand. "That's my number. If you change your mind."

The door slammed open, and Mr. Hastings glared at us from the doorway. "Humph," he muttered. "Ten minutes, sir."

With a charming smile, Mr. Reed said, "Of course, of course."

Doe Eyes grabbed my arm and hustled me from the room. I'd been offered a rescue, and I'd declined it. I was such an idiot. I was going to have to figure out my own way. But at least I'd be dependent on no one but myself. There wasn't anyone else I could trust.

She dumped me back in the dormitory, and I slumped on my cot. The other girls were at recreation, thankfully. I slipped off the fancy dress and put on one of the white nightgowns. Our day wear wasn't much different: plain cotton dresses. I suppose it had something to do with making us look more old-fashioned, like a religious charity, but I missed the feel of jeans and tee shirts. I'd kept the pink unicorn shirt I'd been wearing when I was taken under my pillow for a few years, but eventually one of the other girls had stolen it. When I complained to one of the wardens, I'd been beaten for holding on to useless things. Our life before was over, and we might as well get used to it, she'd said.

Well, I'd gotten used to it. I barely remembered what my parents looked like. Black hair and dark green eyes like me I supposed. Sometimes I could hear my mother's voice, and I think she used to sing me to sleep. I wondered if they still looked for me, or if I'd been presumed dead. Had they been shifters like me? You'd think if they'd been magical, they'd have had some way to find me. Some tracking skill or something. Maybe *they* were dead.

My heart ached at the thought. Had I still somehow held on to the hope that they were out there? That they'd come and try to rescue me like Mr. Reed? Stupid. That's what Rose would have called me, and she'd have been right.

I slipped under the covers and closed my eyes. Tomorrow was Thursday, laundry day for Hastings House. My best bet of getting out undetected was to climb aboard the truck or hide in the bin. I needed to get on laundry duty.

I could do this on my own. I didn't need Mr. Reed or his promises. My stomach swirled uneasily. *Did I?*

3

Hailey

At some point in the planning process, I must have drifted off to sleep. I'd been running with another wolf in my dream this time, a reddish brown animal. We howled and chased the rabbits across the grass . . . until a sound blared out louder than the howling, and I sat up in bed. Red lights flashed at all the windows. The wardens appeared at the doorways beckoning the girls to follow them. Groups of sniffling children and young women moved toward them, including Cassie and Rose.

I ignored them and ran to the windows. People in blue and white police gear streamed across the lawn under the full moon. The four rottweilers and the guards had been lined up to the side of the drive. Metal cages held the dogs, and the guards kneeled with their hands at their backs. Why had the cops come? Had someone reported what this place really was? Had Mr. Reed? My heart knocked against my rib cage. Glancing back at the wardens and the girls departing the room, I grinned. I didn't really care why the police were here. This was my chance.

I yanked a navy blue dress over my nightgown and pulled on some shoes. Looking around, I was glad I had no possessions. Nothing to take. Nothing to worry about. I ran to the window and unhooked the latch. I'd learned to climb the metal piping almost from the moment I'd arrived. It was always good to have an escape route. I'd shown Cassie when she first turned up too, but she'd been too frightened to try it.

Clamping down on my useless concern for the other girls, I shimmied down the piping and dove into a nearby bush. The front yard was illuminated by the police cars' flashing lights, and the back was awash with moonlight, but there were plenty of hiding places for those who knew the territory. Rabbits and squirrels darted ahead of me, running from the wolf who still lurked within.

I hid in bushes and behind trees as I picked my way across the side and front yard. It helped that the police were focused on the main house. A policewoman wandered close to my bush with her flashlight out, but I waited, still and silent, until she passed. I held my breath as the scent of her sweat and nervousness tripped over me. She must be new.

As soon as she was gone, I took off for the main gate. It was wide open. I grinned, tasting freedom for the first time in my life.

Glancing back and forth, I darted through the gate and down the gravel drive to the main road. There weren't any other houses nearby, much of the property around us was undeveloped.

When I reached the main road, I skidded to a stop. The asphalt stretched out in either direction, and I had no idea which might lead to town and which didn't. Beyond the road, woods continued up the hill, and the moon hung low in the sky.

A howl echoed down through the trees, and my wolf eyes could just make out the blur of red on the wooded slope. The red wolf was real? Was he Mr. Reed or some other wolf who'd heard me? I stepped toward him, onto the blacktop.

When I'd run with the wolves in my dreams, I'd been free. Finally able to choose what and who I could to be, I knew that's what I wanted. I wanted to smell the fresh pine and hunt rabbits and dance under the stars. Tears wet my cheeks, and I took another step toward the red wolf.

Roaring filled my ears as a dark car sped toward me. I froze, blinking at the over-bright headlights. The car skidded to a stop in front of me, and the door flung open.

"Get in," Mr. Reed hollered.

I frowned at him and glanced back at the slope. "But the red wolf?"

"He's here?" Mr. Reed asked, scanning the forest behind himself.

He smelled like fear, like the rookie cop I'd run across earlier. Why would another wolf shifter scare him? Weren't they all on the same team?

Loud voices came from the path behind me.

"I see her!" a man shouted, and boots crunched gravel.

"Get her," said another.

Mr. Reed held out a hand. "Please, Hailey, get in."

Glancing back and forth between the police and the red wolf, I grimaced and climbed into the sleek sports car. I'd barely closed the door when Mr. Reed slammed on the gas and we were in motion. The wheels squealed on the pavement, and I smelled the burned rubber.

Looking back through the window, I saw the police officers running towards their cars. They'd never catch us. My gaze was tugged back to the forest. *But he might.*

"Who is the red wolf?" I asked, squeezing and releasing my hands in my lap.

"Kaiden Hartsman," Mr. Reed said, staring at the road ahead of us.

He had a death grip on the wheel, which I appreciated, since we hadn't slowed from our hundred miles per hour speed. A hard pit sat in my stomach. I couldn't decide if I wanted to open the window and hang my head out in the breeze or throw up. "And who is he?"

"A very bad . . ." Mr. Reed glanced over at me and then back at the road. "Creature."

"He's a wolf shifter like . . . us?"

Mr. Reed grimaced. "Not exactly."

I frowned. How was Kaiden different? "What is he?"

"The headmaster will explain everything when you are safely ensconced in Thornbriar Academy. Right now, we need to lose him."

I glanced back through the rear window. "Is he following us?"

Mr. Reed nodded tightly. "I expect so." He exhaled. "But we can outrun him; he's on foot."

"Did you call the police?"

"No."

My eyebrows drew together. I had been sure it was a distraction so he could rescue me after all. Biting my lip, I hoped the police freed the other girls and took them home. Especially Cassie. She hadn't been gone so long that her parents would have stopped looking. "Were my parents shifters?"

"Likely," he said. "Now hush. I have to concentrate."

We took a sharp turn out of the woods and into town. The car slowed as we joined the flow of traffic. There seemed to be a festival going on, as some roads were blocked and large groups of people gathered around tents pitched on the green spaces. Music spilled from the tents, and I grinned. I wanted to jump out and dance. It'd been so long since I'd done something for fun.

Looking down at my dress, torn from my run through the bushes, I frowned. I'd be instantly recognizable. "I wish I had other clothes."

Mr. Reed snorted and gestured toward the back seat. "I grabbed something for you in the back."

Climbing over the seat into the back, I opened the bag and stared at the ragged jeans and tee shirt. I couldn't help the grin that spread over my face as I slipped on the clothes. He hadn't included a bra or panties so I had to keep the scratchy ones from Hasting's House, but it was worth it. The feel of real blue jeans and soft jersey was amazing. Even if they were old and shabby, I felt like a real girl again.

"There're sneakers in there too," he said, eyes still on the road as he dodged drunk pedestrians.

I pulled out the well-loved sneakers and socks and kicked off the impractical ballet slippers. My feet felt heavier with them on, but sturdier. I could run and run in these. The thought settled into me, and I knew what I had to do.

When the car jerked to a stop at a red light, I flung open the door and hopped out. I took off through the crowd, dodging the dancers, and headed into the thickest section of the partygoers. The smell of fried chicken, beer, and sweaty humans assaulted my nose, but I only laughed. I was free. My toes picked up the beat, and I started to dance, my long black hair swirling around me. Closing my eyes, I allowed the music to soak into me.

A man jostled me, and my eyes snapped open.

"All alone out here, sweetheart?" he asked. His fat chin was dotted with whiskers.

My wolf growled, and he blinked stupidly at me.

"I'm always up for partying with a pretty young thing like you." Swinging an arm around my shoulders, he tried to pull me toward him. Alcohol fumes washed over me, and I gagged.

Kicking out with my foot, I slammed his shin, and he fell forward. With a gasping breath, I shoved my palm against the tip of his bulbous nose. Blood gushed over my hand and he squealed, backing away.

I smiled after him, satisfied. I wasn't easy prey.

A hand came down on my shoulder, and I turned, ready to attack again. I met Mr. Reed's gaze.

"That's enough," he said with an unyielding tone.

My heart beating rapidly with the adrenaline, I kicked out toward his shin. Faster than I could blink, he grabbed my throat with his other hand. Snarling, I stared up at him. My entire body thrummed with the need to strike out, to assert my dominance.

He squeezed my throat just a little bit, letting me know that he could cut off my air supply. I bowed my head slightly and cast my gaze to the ground.

"Let's go," he grumbled, released my neck, and grabbed my arm instead. He yanked me out of the festival and down a dark street to his black sports car. This time he pushed me into the backseat and clicked the child safety locks. Then, he climbed in the front and sped away toward the highway.

I stared at the white lines on the road. Trapped. *Again.*

"I'm doing this for your own good," Mr. Reed said with a sigh. "You need what Thornbriar can teach you."

I pressed the button on the door, and the window rolled down half-way. The cool night breeze rolled over me. From one kind of imprisonment to another. It didn't feel much different to me.

4

Hailey

A s the car rode along—at a saner speed—I must have fallen asleep, because the next thing I knew I was being hustled on board a small airplane. "Where are we?"

"On our way to the academy," Mr. Reed said, pushing me into a seat and then sliding into the adjacent one.

Facing us was a woman in a green suit with kind amber eyes. Her black curls had been cut close to her head, but it didn't make her look severe the way the wardens did. I wondered sleepily if she was a kind of warden for Thornbriar Academy and if maybe her eyes weren't as kind as they looked.

"Did we lose him?" I asked.

The woman's gaze darted sharply to Mr. Reed, and I smelled the whiff of fear. Why did the red wolf scare these people so badly? What had he done?

Mr. Reed patted my hand. "Yes. He's gone."

I leaned back in the warm leather seat and closed my eyes again.

* * *

What seemed like seconds later, Mr. Reed shook me awake. I growled at him, but he laughed good-naturedly and placed a tray of hot food in front of me. When I caught the scent of steak and mashed potatoes, saliva pooled and I grabbed the silver fork.

Mr. Reed grinned at me as I shoveled the food in my mouth. When I finished, he handed me an embroidered cloth napkin. The letters "TB" were monogrammed in gray and green on the lower right corner.

Thornbriar Academy. I shivered. I hadn't had any education at Hastings House. The last time I went to school, I'd been in the first grade. I was lucky that I knew how to read and write. My mother had been a big reader, and she'd encouraged my love of books. I'd read anything I could get my hands on at Hastings House: newspapers, cereal boxes, and a few random books the wardens left lying around. Doe Eyes had been partial to murder mysteries, and Hawk Nose liked romances. *Go figure.*

Still, other than a decent vocabulary, I'd be way behind the other students, both magically and academically. "How old do kids usually start Thornbriar?"

The woman smiled, her red lips bright against her brown skin. "Children are enrolled at fourteen or fifteen—"

My face must have fallen, because her smile wavered.

"But they stay until they turn twenty-one and we can be sure that they have control over their shift and their beasts."

Twenty-one? My heart sank. Three more years of imprisonment before I could go free? No way. I wouldn't allow myself to be held captive again.

"It's not a prison, Hailey," Mr. Reed said.

Had he read my mind? Crossing my arms over my chest, I asked, "Will I be allowed to leave?"

Shoulders slumping, he shook his head. "Not until we can be assured that you have control over your beast and you've learned the basics of our world."

"Sounds like jail to me," I snarled.

Turning my back to them, I stared out over the clouds. Mountain caps poked through them, and, where the puffy whiteness thinned, I could see dark green forests below us. Miles and miles of wilderness. Would I feel free there?

I felt the warmth of a body close to my shoulder, and the woman said, "Thornbriar Academy is situated in the Blue Ridge Mountains."

"Those are on the east coast, right?" I said, surprising myself by the awe in my tone. I'd never been in the mountains before. Hastings House had been in a cold and hilly area, but nothing so large. They were really beautiful. Before I was taken, I lived in Florida, near the beach. I remembered because I loved to play in the water, but I'd never learned to swim.

"Yes," she said. "It's beautiful country."

I nodded. Turning my face toward her, I asked, "Who are you?"

"Professor Frank," she said, holding out a hand.

I frowned at her hand for a moment, then I shrugged and shook it. "Nice to meet you. You work at Thornbriar?"

"Yes, I teach control to new shifters. Mr. Reed thought I might be of help to you."

Glancing over at him, I smiled wryly. Of course he did. He thought I was too wild. "I haven't shifted yet."

"Most don't until after they turn eighteen, but the techniques of control and management are good to learn at any time." She leaned back in her seat. "Even for humans. They call it: meditation."

That didn't sound so bad. "Will it relieve the itch?"

She smiled. "Somewhat. It helps it be more manageable. We encourage physical outlets too especially for those approaching their first shift."

"Physical?" My eyebrows drew together.

"Exercise such as running, weightlifting, sports, dance, and so on."

I grimaced. We'd gotten plenty of physical activity doing chores at Hastings House, and it hadn't helped much. I thought of the green forests we passed over. Maybe a good long run in one of those would make a difference. "Are we able to leave the campus?"

"No farther than the property line," Professor Frank said. "But that encompasses many acres of woods, so there's lots of room to roam."

My mouth dropped open. "Did you read my mind?"

She chuckled. "No, Hailey, we aren't mind readers."

"Good."

"But it's not hard to know what's on a young wolf's mind. I've had a lot of experience."

"You don't seem old."

"Well, thank you, though I am in human years around seventy."

My eyes widened.

"The magic that makes us shifters gives us longer lives than humans." Her eyes darkened. "But it doesn't make us invulnerable to physical or magical attack."

"Is it dangerous at the Academy?" I didn't like the squeak that slipped into my voice, but there was nothing I could do about it. Hastings House had been horrible, but I knew the dangers there.

"No, no." She shook her head. "You'll be perfectly safe at Thornbriar Academy."

The question hung in the air between us: would I be safe outside of it? I wasn't sure I wanted to know the answer right now. The way they had reacted to the red wolf, to Kaiden Hartsman, told me there were dangers, and I had no idea what they were. Part of me longed to be free, but part of me also wanted to be protected. I could handle human dangers, as I had the man at the festival, but what about shifter ones? I had no idea this world even existed until a few days ago. How was I going to make my way in it?

I glanced over at Professor Frank. She seemed nice, but so did Doe Eyes at first. How could I know who to trust? I swallowed.

The plane jerked, and static echoed from the speaker. The captain said, "We're beginning our descent into Thornbriar now, folks. Buckle up and enjoy the ride."

I hadn't removed my seat belt, but Mr. Reed and Professor Frank buckled themselves in. The air around the mountains was choppier than it had been before, and the small craft shook as we descended.

Looking out the window, I got my first glimpse of Thornbriar Academy. Surrounded by mountains and forests, the buildings of the school rose like old castles I'd seen in pictures. The roofs looked blue in the evening light. Their slanted tops mimicked the pine forest that surrounded them.

The plane landed on a strip a fair distance down the mountain, and when we climbed out, I looked up trying to make out the school through the trees. I couldn't see it. "How far are we from the academy?"

"Not far," Professor Frank said with a reassuring pat on my arm.

We crossed the tarmac in a huddle because the wind had picked up and bundled ourselves into a car. The driver loaded Mr. Reed and Professor Frank's things in the back, and then we headed up the hill. The road had tighter and tighter turns as we reached the top. The clouds seemed to drift toward us in the breezy air. Trees clustered along the roadside, leaving little room if a vehicle came down at the same time we were going up.

I opened and closed my mouth a few times, trying to pop my ears to relieve the pressure. I'd never been up so high before. My family's home had been on the beach at sea level, and Hastings House on no more than small hills. My eyes widened as we came to the iron gates, embellished with the letters TB for the school, surrounded by swirls of artfully made briars and brambles. The gates swung open automatically at our approach.

The drive was smoother after the gate. Had the roughness of the previous road been meant to discourage travel up the mountain? Ahead of us was the front of the school, an imposing stone building with a blue-toned roof. Beyond it, I could just see the roof of another building rose slightly higher against the mountain and after that one, a third stood. Tall towers climbed either end of the building closest to me. My mouth continued to hang open at the sheer beauty of it. Hastings House was large—some might say grand—but it wasn't as big as this nor as impressive.

"Long ago, it was used as a monastery," Professor Frank said. "Some claim to still hear the monks singing in the chapel."

"It's beautiful," I said as we climbed out of the vehicle. Mr. Reed and the driver gathered the bags.

"Although it's been modernized since that time," she continued.

"Thank God," Mr. Reed said with a wink. "I need a shower."

I stumbled to a stop before the stone steps. Looking back and forth, I didn't see anyone else around, but I mumbled, "Will we see other students right now?"

"Why yes," Professor Frank said.

I ran my hands through my black hair. It was a mess, and my clothes weren't new or even fresh. I was exhausted, and I'm sure I had huge dark circles under my eyes. I grimaced. I hadn't even wanted to come here, and now I was worried what they'd think of me? But I was already behind in academics; I didn't need to be seen looking feral on top of it.

It isn't like you're going to stay here long, I told myself. I wouldn't be held prisoner again.

Might as well get this over with then. With a resigned sigh, I moved forward onto the first of the stone steps. The moon shone overhead. It was late. Maybe they'd all be asleep. But as I climbed, I heard voices calling across the school, echoing against the stone walls.

5

Hailey

The main doors opened onto a long hallway. Red carpets stretched over stone floors, and curling wrought-iron staircases stood on either end. I followed Mr. Reed left down the hall, passing three double doors that stood open to the courtyard. The space outside held several gardens, trees, and stone benches, as well as students. Near the door, several boys sat on a bench, laughing and talking. A group of girls clustered nearby winding their long hair around their fingers and chatting.

I froze, staring at them. I was suddenly aware of the blood still clinging to my skin from the festival man's nose.

The girls had been laughing over something, and when they caught sight of me, they laughed harder. One of them stood, flipping her blonde hair back and sauntered over to the edge of the courtyard. Her short blue dress perfectly matched her eyes.

A tingling feeling swept across my neck and face.

Her sharp eyes studied me from head to toe. Hand on her hip, she spun away and asked, "Wonder what the cat dragged in?"

The girl's friends tittered.

I growled low in my throat.

"Or maybe the dog?" she said, returning to their group. They laughed harder. Some of the other girls pointed and whispered.

"Now, Hailey." Professor Frank put her hand on my elbow, and I shook her off, snarling.

I'd dealt with plenty of mean girls at Hastings House. Cowing them had only been a matter of time. It would be the same here.

Taking a breath, I glanced across the courtyard and met the topaz eyes of a boy sitting near the fountain. A sense of quiet and calm flowed through me. I blinked. I'd never felt anything like that before. I forgot all about the blonde, my eyebrows drawing together.

"Come on," Mr. Reed said, and I let him guide me away.

Professor Frank and Mr. Reed hurried me on toward the spiraling staircase, and we followed it up three floors. The headmaster's office sat at the end of a long hall. It must have been inside one of the two towers I'd seen from outside. The solid door, painted red, had an old-fashioned knocker affixed to it.

Mr. Reed knocked on it three times, and the door opened.

The woman who stood by the desk looked younger than Professor Frank. Her chestnut hair tied in a loose bun, she wore a green silk blouse and gray slacks. When she turned toward us, she smiled, displaying perfect teeth and the slight curve of fangs on either end. I couldn't help the gasp that escaped my lips.

"Headmaster Larkin," Mr. Reed intoned in as formal a voice as I'd ever heard from him. "This is Hailey."

She moved with an easy grace across the room and took my hands in hers. "So pleased to meet you, my dear."

I couldn't help my answering smile. I didn't know if it was magic or just natural charisma, but one simply couldn't be impolite to this woman. "Thank you, Headmaster."

"Come sit." She gestured for the three of us to take chairs clustered around a small table. Tea and biscuits were laid out, and she pressed a cup into my hands.

The warmth seeped into me, and I held on to it. There was something different about this woman. It wasn't just her visible fangs, but the paleness of her skin and the grace of her walk. Without thinking, I blurted, "What are you? Are you a wolf shifter too?"

Professor Frank started to apologize, and the headmaster waved her off.

"I hear that you are new to our world," Headmaster Larkin said with another smile. "I am an air shifter which means that I am both a vampire and able to take the form of a hawk."

"A vampire?" I squeaked. "You drink blood?"

"Yes, I need blood for sustenance," she said, lifting her teacup. "But I can also eat whatever human food takes my fancy."

"Even garlic?" I leaned forward. Part of me was terrified, but another part found the whole idea fascinating.

Mr. Reed snorted, and his teacup rattled in his hands.

"Italian food is one of my favorite cuisines." She tilted her head and studied me. "Now, Mr. Reed tells me you are an earth shifter, possibly a wolf."

"Possibly?" I looked back and forth between them. "Are there other kinds? I mean, other kinds of shifters?"

"Yes," the Headmaster said, setting down her cup. "Shifters derive their powers from the elements: air, earth, water, fire."

Not only were shifters real, but now there were more than one kind. I scratched my neck. What had she meant by *possibly* a wolf? I frowned. But hadn't Mr. Reed said something about bears? "So what element does a wolf use?"

"Earth."

I wrinkled my forehead. "And all earth shifters are wolves?"

"Not necessarily. Our power comes from our element, but it can take different forms. Earth shifters tend to be large predators: bears, wolves, or big cats."

"And water?"

"Water shifters transform into large sea animals like sharks, seals, and the like." She tilted her head. "But they also have a humanoid form. I guess you might call it a mer-person."

"Like a mermaid?"

She nodded. "And fire shifters become a kind of rock creature. They are very strong and not easily hurt. Although . . ." She pursed her lips. "Also not easily healed."

"And air shifters are vampires and . . . birds?"

"Just so."

It made an odd kind of sense. Trying to force my thoughts into some sort of order, I picked up a scone from the plate. It looked delicious: blueberry and coated with extra sugar. I could always count on my stomach to distract me, especially during a wolf phase.

Why had I had all those dreams about flying and swimming and breathing fire? They sounded a lot like the other shifter forms. Did everyone have those dreams? I wanted to ask, but something told me not to. I didn't know these people well enough yet.

Her eyes on my face, Headmaster Larkin asked, "And you've been living in an orphanage of sorts?"

Taking a bite, I moaned. The scone was just as good as it looked. Through my chewing, I said, "Yes, I was kidnapped when I was seven."

"You remember your parents?"

"A little." I rubbed my chest. "We lived in Florida near the beach."

"Must have been lovely," she said, sipping her own tea. "Do you recollect your parents' names? Your last name?"

Her intensity had increased with the latest questions. They seemed especially important to her. I set down the teacup and looked directly at the Headmaster. "No, no idea."

She sighed. "That's a shame."

I nodded and wondered if she could tell I was lying.

* * *

After I met with the headmaster, Professor Frank took me to the girls' dorm. I guess she felt it best to avoid the courtyard because we traveled through quiet hallways. I ran my hand along the smooth stone walls and looked up at the odd contrast of the electric lighting.

"Thornbriar is kind of a square," Professor Frank said. "Administration and the library up front. Girls' and boys' dorms in the back."

"Separate dorms?" I asked, trying to be interested while I rubbed my eyes. It really had been a long trip.

"Of course." She smiled. "Although visiting is allowed during the daylight hours."

I never understood things like curfews. How was the night really more dangerous than the day? Especially in a school of shifters and vampires? But I guessed those were the school rules. I swallowed. "What other rules are there?"

"Oh Hailey," she chuckled. "You don't really have to worry about all that right now."

I frowned. "Tell me."

She shrugged. "Just the usual kind of school things. Do your work. Be on time. No fighting. Stay inside the property lines."

They all sounded reasonable, but my skin itched at the last one. I really was in another cage. *Perhaps a more gilded one,* I thought looking at the furnishings, *but still a prison.*

We stopped in front of a plain white door in the girls' dorm.

"You share a suite with three other girls," Professor Frank said, flipping through keys on a ring. "There's a common room, and then each of you has a separate bedroom."

My own room. I blinked. I didn't remember ever having my own room.

Had I had my own room when I lived with my parents? I remembered the quiet roll of the waves outside and the barking of the neighbor's dog. I brushed the memories away. There was so little I had from that time. I hadn't even been willing to give the headmaster my last name, as if telling her stole it from me. As if her saying, 'oh yes, a fine shifter family' or 'no, I've never heard of them' would make them somehow less mine.

The lounge was dark and quiet, and the other bedroom doors were closed. Professor Frank opened the last door on the right and flipped on the light.

Really, as far as bedroom spaces go, it was tiny, but it was all mine. My heart swelled. I walked across the room, peered out the window and sank down on the cushiony mattress. A bed. A real bed. The sheets and bedding were all gray and green, school colors.

The professor rustled through some drawers and pulled out some clothes. "Pajamas," she said. "School provided."

Of course. My lip curled in disgust. It was still a jail, and they had to make sure all the inmates looked the same.

She smiled. "I'll leave you to get settled then. I'll send someone in the morning to help you sort out your class schedule and all the rest."

"Thank you," I said, and the professor ducked out the door. I stared at the wallpaper covered in tiny, red roses. They'd finished these rooms for comfort, I guessed, leaving the stone for the hallways. The roses made me think of the closet at Hastings House. Had it been only a few days ago when I was imprisoned in those walls? Trying desperately to control my wolf, and not lose my mind?

A wind brushed past me, and I realized the window was open. Crossing over to it, I stared out. A full moon lay heavy and low over the landscape, illuminating the long yard and fence and the forest that lay beyond. A wolf howled in the distance, and my wolf shifted uneasily inside me.

The last few days of travel and learning had left me exhausted. I could drop right now and fall asleep. But another part of me worried. I'd had a taste of freedom, and I wasn't ready to give it up yet. I looked down at my borrowed clothes. I could run now, before Thornbriar Academy got its grip on me.

Perhaps there were things I needed to learn here. Probably more books than I'd ever seen before. I'd be able to find out what it meant to be a shifter and what form I really turned into. I didn't think anyone went hungry here. I'd be safe.

I'd been safe at Hastings House too. My gut rolled uneasily. Well, as safe as one could be as a captive in a whorehouse. I didn't want safety. I wanted liberation. Looking across the nighttime forest, I could feel the dirt under my feet. I imagined the wind whipping through my hair as I ran. Even if I was hungry, even if I struggled, wouldn't that be better than this imprisonment? Would anyone even notice that I'd gone? I bit my lip, turning to the door. They wouldn't, and I'd be free.

The wolf called again from the forest, and I whispered, "I'm coming."

6

Terrin

Long after Professor Frank and Mr. Reed rushed the new girl away, I couldn't get her out of my mind. She was like a wild thing of the forest with her black hair and her emerald green eyes. Her instant growl when Greta, being herself, tossed the first volley, made my inner jaguar purr. I'd always enjoyed a strong female.

My cat side also fancied her physique. Her body was made for sex with her full breasts and curvy hips. The big cat clawed against my skin, and I ached. I smashed the feelings down and tried to concentrate on the conversation around me. But our shifter natures are not so easily denied, and I fidgeted in my seat.

"Y'all ready for a run?" Sciro's southern drawl slipped out sometimes when he wasn't paying attention.

"Yeah." I jumped at the chance. My brother's vampire nature couldn't resist the moonlight, and Adrian would come if we went, even though he, being a water shifter, preferred to swim. We weren't officially pack brothers yet, but we might as well have been. The three of us had migrated toward each other our first year at Thornbriar and the bonds were unbreakable now.

Heading out through the back gate, we broke into a run as soon as we hit the yard. The smell of the forest and the pumping of my legs was enough to distract my cat. Sciro ran like the wind, outpacing both me and Adrian, but we didn't care.

We had all turned eighteen this year and it was just a matter of time before the others made their first shifts. I'd shifted early, no doubt due to my grandmother's influence. Transformations before eighteen were rare, and there'd been some jealousy from other students. If they'd known what I had to go through to shift early, they wouldn't be so interested. Grandmother's training had been intense.

Still, it didn't bother my brothers. They'd been having dreams about their other forms and feeling them inside for so long, sometimes it felt like they'd already shifted.

When we finally rounded back to the main campus, we were all dripping in sweat. Our muscles sang with exhaustion. Using my shirt to dry the sweat from my brow, I caught sight of a small figure running across the yard.

"Hey, Terrin, you coming?" Adrian asked.

"In a minute," I said, my eyes following the girl. I waved the guys on. "Go ahead, I'll catch up."

"Sure you will," said Sciro. "Like you caught up on the trail?"

They laughed as they headed inside, and I ignored the good-natured ribbing.

Slipping through the shadows I followed the girl. My cat perked up at the smell of her—like lavender—on the breeze. My grandmother kept a pot of it on the windowsill when I was growing up. A friend had brought it back from Greece, she'd said.

By the time I got across the yard, the girl was halfway up the front fence. I leaned against the tree nearest to her and asked, "Going somewhere?"

She froze, her eyes wide and frightened, as she looked around for where the voice had come from. Wild and fierce, yet terrified. She was more like a feral cat than anything.

"It's okay," I said, moving forward slowly, my hands up in an innocent gesture.

When she saw me emerging from the shadows, her eyebrows drew together. "What do you want?"

I raised an eyebrow. "Just wondering when you were going to get to the electrified part of that fence."

Her eyes darted up to the top of the ironwork, and when she found the small wires, her shoulders slumped. She hopped back down to the ground.

Before I even thought about it, I reached out a hand toward her arm. As soon as I touched the bare skin, two things happened. She turned, snarling, and a tingling sensation spread up my arm.

"Whoa," I said, holding my hands out in front of me. "I was only . . ." *Trying to comfort you* sounded stupid. "Seeing if you were okay."

She stared at me as if dumbfounded. Then, she sighed and said, "I'm fine. I only wanted . . ." She looked up toward the trees and the moon.

"To be free?" I asked. I don't know what made me ask it, but I knew a little something about captivity.

She met my eyes and said, "Yeah."

"There's trails over there." I looked down at the sweat still soaking through my tee shirt. "Sometimes a good run . . . it feels . . ."

"It's a release," she said, nibbling on her lip.

My breath caught at the simple sexiness of it. "Uh . . . yeah." I scratched my neck and grinned sheepishly. "Do you want me to show you?"

"Some other time," she said. "I should go back."

"I'm Terrin," I said.

She smiled. "Hailey."

"Nice to meet you," I said. "Welcome to Thornbriar. It's not such a bad place."

"Thanks." She glanced back through the fence with longing on her face, then she turned back toward the building.

"Want me to walk you to your dorm?" I asked.

She shrugged as if it didn't matter to her, but I suspected it mattered more than she would ever admit. Few people had been kind to this girl. I just wanted to wrap her in my arms and protect her forever. Not that I was good at that. My lack of any living family was proof enough. My skills as a defender were minimal at best. She deserved someone better, but at Thornbriar I might be all she had.

7

Hailey

As soon as my head hit the pillow, I was out. Still in my wolf phase, I must have dreamt the usual rabbit chasing dreams, but I woke with no memory of them. I was bone tired from recent events, and it wasn't like things were going to get any easier. Today was my first day of classes at Thornbriar.

I'd barely seen my dorm room last night other than to wonder how I got a whole room to myself. I found myself oddly missing the snoring of the other girls. The space was small, but fully stocked with a bed, a desk, and a couple of small lamps. A closet was built into the wall and filled with clothes.

A knock sounded on the door.

Slipping out of bed, I ran a hand through my hair to try and tame it. I opened the door to find a girl smiling at me. She had curly brunette hair and wide blue eyes, but the clothes she wore were the same gray and green colors as the pajamas I'd donned last night.

"Hi," she said brightly. "I'm Monica Gray."

"Uh, hi."

"Professor Frank said you might need some guidance this morning, and I volunteered."

I nodded.

She gestured to the other doors. "This is our suite. The four of us each have our own rooms, but we share a bathroom there." She pointed to the last door on the left.

"You'll want to get up pretty early or shower at night, because Jocelyn takes forever." Monica rolled her eyes. "You'll find some clothes in your closet, but you can buy anything else you want with your stipend."

My eyes went wide. "I get money?"

She smiled benevolently. "All the scholarship kids do. For clothes and gear and stuff."

"Oh." I glanced down at her plaid skirt and blouse. "Are you a scholarship kid?"

Monica snickered. "No, I'm a Gray."

My face must have looked as baffled as I felt.

With a sigh, she said, "The Grays are kind of famous. My father sits on the Council."

"That's like the ruling government, right?"

"Well, Hailey no-last-name, you've got a lot to learn." Monica scowled. "Grab a shower and get dressed, and I'll show you to the dining room."

"Okay." I closed the door on Monica and sighed. This day was going to be a lot harder than I thought.

I rubbed my head, where an ache was already blooming, and opened the closet. A white robe hung on the back of the door, with a school patch on the breast. Hanging on the bar were school uniforms: plaid skirts and white tops. In the three drawers at the bottom lay pajamas and two unopened packages of underwear and bras. Ugh. Still no jeans.

Glancing over I looked wistfully at the jeans and shirt Mr. Reed had picked up for me, but I needed to try to fit in here. For at least as long as I stayed. Running my teeth along my lip, I slipped out of my pajamas and into the robe. A hot shower would feel amazing. All the supplies for washing were in a little kit at the edge of my desk.

After the shower, I grimaced and put on the school uniform. It fit well at least, although I didn't know how they'd known my size. The shoe choices were slim: sturdy Mary Janes or sneakers. I chose the Mary Janes for now and was surprised to find that they too were the correct size.

Monica was waiting for me in the room outside. The four bedrooms lined a large living space with a couch, a TV, and a small kitchen area with a mini fridge.

"Couldn't I just eat breakfast here?" I mused.

She cocked her head. "No, silly. The whole point of the dining hall is to see and be seen."

Monica wore the same school uniform I did, but she really wore it. The top two buttons on her blouse were undone and her skirt seemed slightly shorter than mine. Her curly hair was pulled back on top and tied with a matching ribbon.

"Do we have to wear uniforms?" I asked.

"Okay, Debbie Downer," she said. "No, after we turn eighteen, we are not required to wear the uniform. But it shows school spirit."

I shrugged. Whatever. "Let's go eat."

Monica led me out of the suite and down the hall. We descended a stone stairwell with some other students. The dining hall was on the first floor of the next building and mealtimes were staggered for the lower and the upper school, Monica explained as we walked.

We passed through the same courtyard that I'd seen the night before from a different direction. There were students clustered here and there on stone benches or lying in the grass. Some had brought their meals out into the early morning sunshine.

The double doors to the dining hall swung open as we approached. Two gorgeous guys came through. One with golden hair and a long sinewy body, and the other was Terrin from last night.

His topaz eyes stared intently at me, and I caught my breath. He was solidly built, but he moved gracefully like a cat. His black hair curled against his head, and his coppery skin appeared smooth to the touch. My hand lifted, and I caught myself, yanking it back to my body.

Forcing my eyes to look away, I studied his friend. He had an easy smile, but there was a tightness to his full lips. I wondered what worried him. They both wore the button-down white shirts of the school uniform and jeans. I grinned. Guess not everyone was into school spirit as much as Monica.

Terrin's friend glanced up and caught my smile. He grinned back, and his whole face lit up. He had green eyes, as deep as the ocean, and an angular nose. He was beautiful and he knew it.

A hand slammed into my back, and I stumbled. Tripping over my own feet and the unfamiliar shoes, I lurched into a broad chest. Hands came up as if to catch me and shoved me to the ground instead.

"What the hell?" growled a deep male voice.

Blinking, I looked up into the most startlingly handsome face, and my words caught in my throat. Dark auburn hair, blue eyes, and chiseled features sat atop a muscled physique. No school uniform for this guy, just a soft jersey tee shirt and black jeans.

"Watch where you're going," he said, his eyes hard. A bit of fire blazed in their stormy depths.

"I'm sorry," I said, stumbling a bit over the words. What was the matter with me? I never acted like this.

He sneered, "I don't need your apologies, new girl."

My heartbeat chittered against my chest. Why was he doing this to me?

Planting his legs wide, he loomed over me and glowered. "Are you just going to lay there?"

"Leave her alone, Brenton," said a familiar voice next to me. Terrin's warm hand slipped into mine and helped me to my feet.

I looked back and forth between two guys who couldn't be more different. Terrin's calm support and Brenton's almost scorching anger, and for the first time in my life, I felt helpless. My cheeks grew hot, and tears threatened. Even when I'd been trapped in Hasting's House, I knew I was strong and I could fight back. What was wrong with me?

Glancing around at the other students laughing and gawking, I caught sight of Monica, her lips boasting a vainglorious smirk. Right behind her stood the girl from last night, her arm across Monica's shoulders.

I pressed my lips together. These were enemies I knew how to fight. Pushing away from Terrin, I marched across the quad and pulled back my fist. Even though I knew I'd get in trouble, slamming it into pretty Monica's eye was the best thing I'd done since I'd arrived at Thornbriar. She crumpled to the ground, screaming.

I sneered and said, "What, are you just going to lay there?"

8

Adrian

Holy shit! The new chick had punched Monica Fucking Gray! She stood over her like an avenging angel, all fire and brimstone, her hands planted on her perfect hips, and her black hair flowing behind her like a cape. My dick stood instantly at attention.

Although to be honest, it had never taken much to catch his interest. I'd been pretty casually flirting with Monica Gray over the last few weeks, and she'd wanted more. Girls usually did, but I was way too young to settle down to just one chick. Probably why she'd pushed the new girl into that dickhead Brenton.

Still, I adjusted my pants. My pack mate, Terrin had already laid claim to the new girl, no matter what my dick said. He hadn't been able to stop talking about her last night when Sciro and I were just trying to play a video game.

Terrin was gaping at the new girl as we all had been, even, to my surprise, dickhead Brenton. I snorted. Will wonders never cease?

I tapped Terrin on the shoulder and jerked my head in her direction. "Go get her."

He bobbed his head and ambled over toward her. Normally, Terrin was smooth as a jungle cat, but this girl put him on edge. I could feel the tension riding him. It coated the air like a thick smog. I grimaced. She brought out his protective instincts, and in Terrin that wasn't always a good thing. I'd better tag along and make sure he didn't get in too deep. I hurried over to them.

Then I saw it. Every time Terrin traced his hand down her back, the new girl softened. He whispered in her ear, and she relaxed. By the time I'd crossed the short distance to them, he was guiding her back toward the dining hall, a hand on the small of her back.

Shit. I was too late.

9

Hailey

I don't know how he did it, but Terrin's voice made my nerves soften. The anger that had boiled through me seeped away. His possessive hand at the small of my back should have made me furious, but it somehow had the opposite effect. I was safe. Protected. I could relax.

He guided me toward the dining hall, and the eyes of the other students drifted away from us. I took a couple of deep breaths and was rewarded with the smells of eggs and bacon drifting out of the cafeteria. That was it. I was starving. That's why I'd reacted like a weakling.

"Hailey?" asked Professor Frank at the door of the dining hall. Her brown eyes searched me as if she could see all I'd been through in the courtyard.

"I'm okay," I said, and I was.

Her eyebrows drew together. "You attacked a fellow student in the courtyard."

I blinked. Hadn't they seen her shove me? How that guy had screamed at me? "She pushed me."

"That's no excuse for violence," Professor Frank said.

"No." I shook my head. "That's not fair." The Professor's serene voice rubbed against my raw nerves. Where Terrin soothed me, she grated. What was wrong with her? I'd only been defending myself.

Her lips pressed together. "I think you'll need some remedial classes in control."

"What?" I exclaimed. At this rate, I'd be in remedial classes for everything. I was already starting later than any other student.

Terrin stroked my back, rubbing between my shoulder blades, and I exhaled.

Professor Frank's dark eyes sharpened.

I closed my eyes. Was her kind demeanor a sham, just like the wardens at Hastings House? I should have known I couldn't trust anyone but myself. What were the punishments like here? More than remedial classes I expected. Opening my eyes, I said, "I'm sorry. I'll do better."

She searched my face again. "I'll leave you in Mr. Matos' capable hands."

Laying a hand on Terrin's arm, she said, "She's had a rough time of it. I think you know something about that."

He nodded, and we moved into the dining hall. It was like no cafeteria I'd ever seen before. Along the far wall, tables were lined up, covered in gray and green tablecloths. The food on top was laid out as if we were at a buffet, the promised bacon and eggs, as well as french toast, hash browns, and brownies at the end. Terrin guided me along, filling my plate with more than I could ever eat.

"That's too much," I said.

Terrin grinned. "You've been to war. You need to eat like a warrior."

I laughed.

Once my plate was full, he guided me out the back door of the dining hall into a hallway that led toward another building beyond.

"Where are we going?"

"My suite," he said and he must have seen the concern rising on my face, because he put out a hand in a calm down gesture. "I just think

43

you'll be more comfortable in a quiet place away from public stares."

I swallowed. He was right. I wouldn't have been able to eat anything in the courtyard after what had happened, and the dining hall was still busy. I followed him up the stairs into the boys' dormitory. The hall looked similar to the girls, and when he opened the door, I peered into the disaster that was their suite. They had a gray couch just like ours, and a TV, although it was several sizes larger. A mass of cords lay in front of it, hooked up to various gaming systems. The kitchen was overflowing with snack bags and there were dumbbells dumped in one corner. A huge sound system sprawled across one side, with speakers that were almost as big as I was.

Terrin cleared some space on the coffee table and set my food down there. Then, he gestured for me to sit.

The couch was a lot fluffier than I'd imagined, and I sank tiredly into its deep folds. Picking up my plate, I took a bite. The taste was everything the smell had promised, but I forced myself to take slow bites, savoring every bit.

"You want water? Or a Coke?" Terrin asked from the kitchen area, leaning over the mini fridge.

His backside was outlined in his blue jeans, and warmth curled in my gut. I shook myself.

"Coke." Why not? I hadn't had one since before I was kidnapped.

Terrin popped open two soda cans, a tinny sound followed by the gurgle of bubbles. He brought them over and set them on the table, sitting on the couch next to me.

His nearness heated my arm and thigh that were closest to him. I squirmed in my seat. "So, is Terrin a Spanish name?"

"Huh?"

I licked my lips. "Professor Frank called you Matos. Isn't that Spanish?"

"Yes, but Terrin isn't."

"Oh." I was an idiot. What was I doing? Trying to strike up a conversation with this guy, just because he'd been nice to me? I took a couple more bites of food and stared at the carpet.

"Hey," he said, touching my arm. "My birth name was Junio Matos. I chose Terrin myself after coming to Thornbriar. I wanted to put the past behind me."

I nodded. I knew all about that. "Did it help?"

"Sometimes," he said thoughtfully. "You've got to look toward the future because the past will drown you."

I gave him a half-smile.

The door to the suite swung open, and two guys stomped in. One was the Adonis I'd seen Terrin with earlier. The other was a paler-skinned guy with coal black hair. He was just as well-built as the other two, but he didn't look like he'd spent any time in the sun. When they saw me, they both pulled to a stop.

"Hey. Terrin," the pale guy said, "and the new girl."

Terrin growled. "Her name is Hailey." He turned to me. "Hailey, this is Adrian." He gestured toward the blonde. "And Sciro. They're my brothers in all the ways that count."

"Brothers?"

"He means pack, not blood relations," Adrian said as he strolled forward. "Lovely to meet you, Hailey."

I nodded. Words caught in my throat. How could any group of guys command that much beauty? I flushed.

"Nice to meet you," said Sciro. His words frosted as if he wasn't entirely sure it was nice to meet me.

Terrin frowned at him, but didn't say anything more.

"You missed class this morning," Sciro said, crossing to the fridge.

"I was helping Hailey get settled," Terrin said, leaning back into the couch next to me. "She had a confrontation with Greta's crew."

Sciro shrugged. "Doesn't everyone? It's like a bloody school initiation."

Despite the sour way he said it, his comment made me laugh. At least I hadn't been the only one to find the girls mean. They picked on everyone.

Adrian loped over and sat on the arm of the couch, grabbing a bag of chips off the table. "Mr. Reed is still hanging around. He usually drops the recruits and runs."

"That's weird," Terrin said, draping an arm over the couch behind me.

I leaned into his forest scent, then I stopped. What was I doing? I needed to get my feet under me at this school, and here I was hiding out with these—admittedly drop dead gorgeous—guys. "Shouldn't I be in class or something?" I said uneasily. "Monica was supposed to show me around."

"Professor Frank gave me this," Adrian handed me a folded paper.

As I opened the paper, I inhaled Adrian's salt-water scent. It reminded me of home—well, my first home—the beach. A basic class schedule was outlined on it, along with several sessions of "T.A." that all met in the library. "What's T.A.?"

"Tutoring Assistance," Sciro said, curling his lip. "It means you're behind in one or more subjects and need to catch up."

"Oh." My heart sank at the three sessions of T.A. listed on my schedule. I'd only be in regular classes half the day. Even here, I was still a freak.

"Don't worry about it," Terrin said. "I had several sessions when I first started. My grandmother pulled me out of school so much, my education was spotty."

"Your grandmother?" I asked.

"Long story," he said with a shrug. He glanced at the time on the tablet. "Looks like your first session is on the hour. I'd better be getting you to it."

"They are all in the library," Sciro said. "Your classes are on the other side of campus. I'll take her."

Terrin frowned at him, but then he nodded. "You'll take care of her?"

Sciro didn't look happy about it, but he said, "Of course, man."

I set down my empty plate and stood. Glancing back at Terrin, I squared my shoulders. I could do this. Mean girls were my specialty after all those years at Hastings House, and I only had to deal with it until I could find a way to escape Thornbriar that didn't involve electrocuting myself. Still, I shivered at the sudden chill of not having Terrin by my side. I met Sciro's cold blue eyes and forced command into my voice. "Let's go."

He raised a sardonic eyebrow but gestured toward the door and said, "After you, my lady."

10

Sciro

I followed the new chick, Hailey, down the hall of the boys' dorm, kicking myself. When had I turned into such an ass? I was acting worse than that lout Brenton. The problem was I had smelled her the moment I walked into the room. Her scent was a delicious combination of blood and lavender, and all I wanted to do was nick a vein and drink my fill. But even if I'd wanted to make a play, Terrin had been all over her staking his claim. I couldn't do that to my bro.

Shoving my hands in my jean pockets, I watched her ass sway in that ridiculous school skirt. I groaned. While vampires were as hot-blooded as any other shifter, I liked to get to know a girl a bit before we hopped in the sack. And I didn't know anything about this one. None of us did.

"Hailey," I said, forcing some niceness into my tone.

She paused, looking back at me.

I scratched my neck. "I don't mean to be such an ass."

"Really?" She arched a dark eyebrow at me.

I snorted. Boy, she had a mouth on her. Two luscious red lips that came to a perfect bow. I slapped myself mentally. *Sciro. Quit it, you idiot. She's taken. She's Terrin's.*

Gesturing to the halls around us as we descended the stairs, I said, "I hear all this is new to you."

She shrugged.

"What kind of shifter are you?" I asked, trying to stroll casually next to her.

"Is that polite to ask?" she muttered.

"Well, no, not really," I said, bemused. "But I didn't expect you to know that."

A small smile crossed those amazing lips, and my cock strained against my zipper. What would that mouth be like, wrapped around my bulging . . . *damn it!* When did I become such a letch? I shook myself and volunteered, "I'm an air shifter."

She paused her step, studying me with those intense eyes. "Does that mean you are a vampire like Headmaster Larkin?"

"Well, I wouldn't say there's anyone like the Headmaster, but yes, all air shifters are vampires and able to shift into birds."

"Are you dead?"

"Not exactly." I laughed. I'd wondered the same thing in the years since I'd discovered what I was. To my parents I was. As soon as they'd found out I was a vampire, they'd thrown me out on the street. *Filthy, undead, evil creature!*—my father's last words to me as he'd tossed my ass off their property.

I shook myself again. "Vampirism is more like a virus," I quoted Professor Ward. "It's present in the human and shifter populations, but only air shifters are susceptible to its effects."

"Huh, that's weird. What are Terrin and Adrian?"

"Terrin's an earth shifter. He shifts into a black jaguar. He's the only one of us to have transformed so far." I watched her face, trying to gauge her reaction but she was pretty much a blank slate. I wondered if she'd ever been around other shifters before. "Adrian's a water shifter."

She frowned. "But there's no water around here."

I grinned. "There are several saltwater pools in the caverns beneath us." I gestured down. "The creators of Thornbriar wanted to make sure that it felt like home to all shifters."

"Oh."

Her mouth rounded as she spoke, and my cock stirred again. You'd think I was a fucking Casanova like Adrian, responding to every girl who walked by. I gritted my teeth. "And you are?"

"You can't tell?" she asked, looking at her feet.

"No, it's hard to tell without knowing someone really well."

"An earth shifter," she said carefully. "Mr. Reed thinks my form will be wolf."

"Were your parents shifters?"

"I don't know," she said. "I was kidnapped when I was seven and held prisoner until now."

I blinked, a million questions battering at my brain, but I didn't know what to ask first. Many shifters didn't have an easy life, but guys like Terrin and I had it especially rough. At least, I thought we had until I heard this. "Captive? How?"

"A human trafficking ring disguised as a home for wayward girls." Her voice was matter-of-fact, as if this was no big deal.

Shit. I'd lived on the street, and some of the stories I'd heard of the girls and the younger boys getting raped sickened me. She'd lived in a place that sold them off like livestock. How had she stayed sane?

I hadn't even seen the hallways we'd walked, but, suddenly, the library door was before us. Wooden with gold trimmed edges, it shined in the dark hallway. "This is the library."

"Okay," she said, stepping forward.

"Hailey?" I reached out and touched her arm.

She looked at me.

"I'm sorry for what you went through." I grimaced.

"I know," Hailey said, giving me a small smile. "Thank you for showing me the way, Sciro." Then, she opened the library door and stepped through, shutting it behind her.

Staring at the intricate scrollwork, I exhaled. Hailey no-last-name was trouble, pure and simple.

11

Hailey

hy had I said all that to Sciro? I frowned as I closed the library door behind me. I chewed on my lip and turned to look around.

My jaw dropped, and I stared at the beautiful place that was Thornbriar Academy library. Bookshelves covered every wall, stocked with books, but also decorated with lovely gold filigree like that which illustrated the door. Work tables and chairs with slim forest-green cushions dotted the space. Two spiral staircases clustered in the center of the room, leading to even more bookcases on the second floor. Four long, narrow windows stretched ceiling to floor between the bookcases, their heavy green drapes were drawn to the side and letting in filtered daylight.

I crossed to one, and looked out across the campus. The clouds had come in as the morning wore on, and they drifted low, dragging their tails across the buildings.

"Gorgeous, isn't it?" said an older male voice behind me.

Turning, I met the gaze of a professor. He was massive, but all muscle under his gray sweater vest and slacks. I felt very small in his shadow. His rusty brown hair started to gray at the top, and faded tattoos marked his lower arms. I forced a smile. "Yes, it is."

His eyes crinkled as he grinned. "You must be Hailey," he said, offering me a hand.

I took it reluctantly, but he only gave a gentle shake.

"I'm Professor Ward. I'll be your instructor for T.A."

I grimaced.

"No worries," he said, laying his finger alongside his nose. "We'll get you up to speed in no time."

Yes, I could do this. It was just schoolwork, right? I followed Professor Ward into the back of the library. He gestured for me to sit at one of the work tables and handed me a test, a legal pad, and pencil.

"I'm afraid to know where one must go, we need to know where you are. Just a short test on some basics." He set a kitchen timer on the edge of the desk. It was shaped like a rooster. "Fifteen minutes, I think."

He wandered back into a small room nearby, and I heard the clank of dishes. I stared down at the sheets he'd given me. The test was divided into sections for reading, math, history, and science. Taking a breath, I scanned for the easiest questions first and answered those, then I went through the harder ones. Reading was easy as I'd gained a fair amount of vocabulary on my own, and I'd picked up some history, from the warden's more historical romances. But science and math were harder.

When the buzzer went off, the Professor arrived at my desk and held out his hand. I gave him the papers, and he replaced them with a cup of tea. I breathed in the warm cinnamon scent of it and cupped my hands around it. Even on a warm day like today, there was something comforting about tea. My forehead wrinkled as the thought skittered by. It hadn't really come from me. There'd never been much tea at Hastings House, but someone I'd known before had liked it. Maybe my parents.

"Well, young lady," Professor Ward said. "Looks like we have a fair amount of work ahead of us."

I swallowed uneasily.

"But you're a bright girl." He smiled. "And you read well. I'm sure we'll get through it."

Shuffling through a pile of books, he'd stacked next to the table, he pulled out a math textbook. He flipped it open before I could read the cover and laid it down open in front of me. "Let's work on these problems for the next bit, shall we?"

The next few hours whizzed by as we covered some basics in every subject area. When we finished, he handed me a stack of books and told me to read them by the end of the week.

Then, he shooed me off. "Shifter History is waiting."

"But I'm behind there too."

"You need some time with people your own age. I'm sure you'll catch on quickly, Hailey."

Holding my books tight to my chest, I was out the door and down the hall before I realized that I had no idea where my next class was. There was no one in the hallway to ask, so I just wandered back the way Sciro and I had come up.

One of the doors was cracked open, and I heard voices from within. I raised my hand to knock and ask for directions, when I realized who they were talking about.

"Kaiden Hartsman attacked the Council chambers today," said a nasal woman's voice.

I knew that name. The red wolf that chased me and Mr. Reed.

"Oh no, not again!" another female replied.

"Robert Gray was injured," said the nasal one.

"Not Monica's father? The poor girl will be devastated."

"Kaiden is the most dangerous spirit shifter who's ever lived," the nasal one continued. "He needs to be exterminated."

"Well, he should have been. At birth, like the rest of them! What could his parents have been thinking?"

I'd never even heard of this kind of shifter and they killed them? At birth?

The nasal one sighed. "What all parents think. They loved their child and didn't want to sacrifice him."

"And now look at all the shifters who've been sacrificed. To their selfishness."

I stepped back, looking up and down the still empty hallway. Kaiden Hartsman was a spirit shifter? What was that? They'd told me about earth, air, water, and fire shifters but no one had ever mentioned spirit.

Running my teeth over my lip, I turned toward the stairs. Apparently, spirit shifters were killed at birth. Why? Because they were evil? He'd attacked Monica's dad and the Council, whatever that was. I'd heard it mentioned before as some kind of ruling body, but what did they really do?

I was so lost in my thoughts that I slammed into a rock hard chest and fell back on my butt for the second time that day. Looking up, I winced as I stared into stormy blue eyes.

"What, are you blind?" Brenton growled. "Or just an idiot?"

My face burned with embarrassment. Twice in one day? I didn't even have Monica to blame for this one. "I'm sorry. I wasn't looking where I was going."

"Obviously," he said with a sneer. "You'd think you were blonde under all that darkness."

Climbing to my feet, with no help from him, I glared. "I bet you've never made a mistake in your life."

He scowled. "Just get out of my way, new girl." Brenton shoved past me and continued down the hall.

"Hey, could you tell me where . . ." He was gone. *Dammit.* I rubbed my sore butt and headed in the opposite direction. Even if Brenton was going to Shifter History, I didn't want to sit in class with that asshole.

12

Terrin

We were sitting on our usual bench between classes. My eyes darted toward the stairs to the library wing. Hailey should be done with T.A. by now. Every nerve in my body itched to see her, needed her by my side. My cat purred in agreement.

Everything in me called out for me to claim her as mine, but I knew I shouldn't. She deserved better than me. I balled my hands into fists. She needed a protector, and I had never been able to protect what was important to me. Not even my family.

Monica Gray came flying across the courtyard, hair streaming, and slammed into Adrian. His arms came around her instantly, stroking her head. Adrian never had a problem offering comfort to chicks. I wish I knew how he did it.

"What's wrong? Monica?" he asked, his voice low and soothing.

I didn't know why he was always so kind to her. She really was kind of a jerk. This was probably another play to get his attention.

"My father's been injured," she said through her tears. Her whole body trembled.

Now, I felt like a jerk. Adrian and Monica both had family members on the Council. Of course she'd come to him for this.

She sobbed. "Kaiden Hartsman attacked the Council."

All of the hairs on my neck stood up at the name. He had been the bane and terror of all of our lives for so long. A spirit shifter gone rogue and determined to take down the Council.

"Is everyone else okay?" Adrian asked, his voice steady despite the tension I felt riding my brother.

He and his family might not have gotten along, but they were still blood. His mother had served on the Council for several years now, and if she'd been hurt, he'd go ballistic.

"Seven deaths," Monica choked out. "But the only high official to be hurt was Father."

Adrian visibly let his breath out.

His mother was safe then. As much as any of us were safe. Kaiden's attacks had gotten more brutal and more directed over time. He'd recruited the normal law enforcement to assist him and used our people's natural hesitation to expose ourselves and hurt humans to escape capture.

My jaguar growled, clawing against my insides. He wanted to hunt Kaiden Hartsman. Hunting murderers was what cat and I did. He and I were made for this.

I squared my shoulders and took a deep breath. *Not anymore.* Now we stayed out of sight so the people we knew could stay safe. Bloody images shot across my mind's eye and I tried to push them away. *Abuela! Tio!* Their bodies were in pieces. My heart beat frantically against my chest as if I was living it all over again.

Forcing myself to breathe deeply as Professor Frank taught us, I lifted my eyes and gazed across the courtyard. I just needed to get out of my head. To forget the past and move forward as I'd told Hailey.

Hailey appeared at the doorway to the yard. Gorgeous. Fragile. In need of protection. My mouth dried as I stared at her. I couldn't be trusted with something that precious. After everything I'd lost, I couldn't take care of her and I couldn't bear to lose someone else. I stood. My jaguar growled at me. She was ours. He'd claimed her almost instantly.

But I couldn't do it. I had to listen to my rational mind, not my instincts. I couldn't take the chance I'd lose anyone else. I headed back into the building, ignoring everyone.

Her face puzzled, Hailey frowned at me as I passed. I couldn't speak. I couldn't tell her I was wrong for her.

My cat whined and clawed at my skin.

13

Hailey

A couple of days later, I walked into the dining hall at dinnertime. I was still trying to get my legs under me as far as the school went, but wolf phase wouldn't let me miss any meals. The usual suspects were hanging out in the courtyard, but I hadn't seen Terrin or Adrian yet. The way Terrin had been ignoring me for the past few days, I hadn't really expected to.

Heading toward the food line, I caught a whiff of the meatballs and tomato sauce. Everything I'd eaten at Thornbriar had been amazing.

One minute I was strolling and the next I was falling toward the tile floor. Shoving my hands out in front, I caught myself by my forearms and my knees. My breath came out in a little huff.

Laughter echoed in my ears, and the blood rushed to my face. I stared at the black and white tiles.

"Always falling at my feet, aren't you?"

I huffed and looked up into Brenton's sneering face. "Yup, your good looks slay me every time," I muttered, standing. My elbows and knees stung, but I wasn't really hurt.

Glancing behind me, I saw Monica and Greta sitting a few feet behind us. "Guess it was the loathsome twins again."

He arched a sardonic eyebrow. "That's one name for them."

I met his eyes for a moment and thought I saw something there, something other than his usual sneer, but it was gone in a flash.

"Get going, Rosie Posie, before you fall down again." He turned and lumbered away.

Looking over at the giggling faces of Greta and Monica, I really wanted to punch them again, but one of the Professors was probably around here and I'd only get in trouble. I forced myself to go get some food like I'd intended in the first place.

"Hey, Hailey," Sciro said, stepping up next to me, his plate already heaped. "I was going to take my food out to the courtyard. Want to join?"

"Sure." I tossed a roll on top of my spaghetti, grabbed a water bottle, and followed him out into the yard.

Sciro and I dropped down onto a bench. In the garden bed next to us, white flowers with sunny yellow centers bloomed. I inhaled their soft scent.

The sky overhead was cloudy, blocking most of the sun. I blinked at Sciro. "Can you be out in the sunlight?"

He laughed. "Yeah, it's not super comfortable for me to be in bright sun, but I can be out on a cloudy day like today."

I nodded, taking a bite of my food. The flavors of the herbs, oregano and basil, ran over my tongue, and I moaned.

Sciro stared at me.

"What?"

"You'd think you'd never eaten before."

"Nothing this good." I grinned.

He shook his head. "I know that feeling."

I studied his face. "Where are you from?"

"I grew up in Atlanta. But—" He gave a wry smile. "My parents tossed me out when I was thirteen."

"Why?"

"We don't shift until after eighteen, well, most of us, but the blood lust shows up early. Pretty much as soon as we hit puberty."

I frowned. "But weren't your parents shifters?"

"No, I was adopted. My parents were human."

"Oh."

"Yeah, they were also pretty religious. A son who shied away from daylight and wanted to drink blood once in a while spooked them pretty bad. They tried to exorcise me."

"Damn."

"Then they threw me out on the street." He shrugged as if it hadn't been that big a deal. "So, I know what it's like to miss a few meals."

I stayed silent. What did one say to a story like that? Of course, that was probably how he felt when I'd blurted out mine. I bit into the meatball, savoring the hearty spiced meat, and thought of all the meals of oatmeal or soup we'd had at Hastings House.

"Wait a minute," I said. "Most of us don't shift until after eighteen?"

He grinned, his whole face lighting up. "Something Terrin didn't tell you about himself?"

Really there had been a lot Terrin hadn't told me, but I gestured *gimme*.

"Terrin shifted for the first time last year, when he was seventeen."

"Whoa, how?"

Sciro shrugged. "Something to do with his grandmother, I heard. But not really my story to tell. You should ask him."

"He's been avoiding me," I said honestly. "I don't know why."

"I wouldn't worry about it," he said. "Terrin's too smart to avoid a pretty girl like you for long."

I snorted.

14

Hailey

The week had passed in a blur as I adjusted to my new classes. The school seemed rocked by Monica's dad getting injured. As far as I could make out, he was some kind of big wig in shifter politics.

I took three classes with regular students: Shifter History & Politics, Magical Meditation & Focus, and Shifter Biology. In every one, I chose the seat closest to the teacher. I needed to soak up as much knowledge as I could so that when I made my escape, I'd have some basics.

Professor Ward laughed at me in Tutoring Assistance, because I whizzed through every book and demanded more. I was so behind. I wanted every advantage I could get.

Heading into Shifter Biology, I glanced across the room and my stomach soured. I didn't know what I'd done to offend Terrin, but every time I walked into a room, he turned away. In the classes we shared together, he kept his eyes carefully averted the entire time.

They'd put me in the regular version of this class even though they knew it would take me a while to catch up. I didn't have time to play whatever games Terrin was playing. I focused my eyes on Professor Alexander, a tall, African man with grey whiskers along his rich black chin.

Shifter biology covered four forms of shifters: earth, air, water, and fire. It was amazing that creatures that were basically of the same species could be so different. Even if two people had the same affinity, their element could produce very different forms. Fire shifters usually became rock creatures when shifting, but some had been known to take dragon form. The other students had laughed at that, and I took it to mean that dragon shifters were rare.

Professor Alexander didn't mention the fifth element, spirit. Did their biology vary as well? I knew so little about them. But the women I'd overheard earlier had said that Kaiden Hartsman was a spirit shifter and that they were usually killed at birth. That seemed a little extreme. What was so wrong with spirit shifters?

I glanced over at Monica with dark circles under her light blue eyes. She'd still come to class every day, but she often looked as if she'd been crying. Her father's condition hadn't improved, I suspected, although I hadn't overheard anymore conversations to that effect.

After class was dismissed, I gathered my books and headed out the door. Terrin ended up right in front of me and I reached out a hand, tapping him on the shoulder. "Terrin?"

He turned and met my eyes for the first time in days. "Hailey."

My forehead scrunched. "Are you okay?"

"Yeah, just a lot on my mind." His gaze dropped to the floor.

"Do you have a parent on the Council too?"

He shook his dark head. "All my family is dead."

I gasped. I hadn't expected that. These guys had grown up in this world. I'd thought they'd had relatively happy family lives. "I'm sorry."

Terrin shrugged. "It was a long time ago."

I wanted to ask why he'd been ignoring me, but the whole conversation was awkward and uncomfortable. I didn't even know how to bring it up. "Well, sorry for bothering you." I couldn't help the bit of hurt that crept into my tone.

He looked up, touching my arm. "I'm sorry, Hailey. I can't be what you need."

"You can't be what?" I asked, my voice sharp. "A friend? Because that's what I need right now."

Pain shot through his eyes, but I turned and marched away. What was wrong with him? Why would he be nice to me and then not?

* * *

I'd taken to eating dinner in my room and then heading to the library. I avoided almost everyone that way. Tonight was no different, except I had a plan. If my classes weren't going to tell me about spirit shifters, I was going to find out for myself.

The library was quiet tonight. A few other students worked here and there, but they were mostly intent on their studies. I headed for my favorite corner. The moonlight slipped through the curtains and illuminated a small armchair and table. It looked like someone had just shoved them here out of the way, more than an intentional workplace, but it was perfect for my needs. Professor Ward had taken to leaving me a few volumes that might enrich my studies nearby. I glanced at the stack, but it didn't offer a distraction tonight.

Perusing the shelves, I searched for any references to spirit shifters. Even for a library of this size, there wasn't much. Was there some kind of restricted section that had more? I glanced toward Professor Ward's office, but it was closed up tight.

Sitting on the gray armchair, I slipped my feet from my shoes and settled in to read. The first few books had things I already knew. The Council had decreed that spirit shifters be killed at birth. They were too dangerous and too unstable. The accounts of spirit shifters who'd gone crazy and killed their whole family or their communities made me shiver.

I dug deeper into the books, and I found accounts of spirit shifters who were amazing artists, gifted actors, and talented writers. Some of the best of shifter literature was written by spirit shifters. I huffed. Of course spirit shifters were only appreciated when they fit the crazy artist stereotype. I nibbled on my lip and closed the book.

"Studying hard?" a stiff male voice asked.

I glared up at Brenton. He still loomed over me, even when I hadn't crashed into him this time. The chiseled planes of his face were set in hard lines, and I wondered if he ever cracked a smile. "Yes."

He frowned as if I was a puzzle he didn't know how to figure out. "Probably need all the help you can get."

"You offering?" I blinked at him innocently.

A snort echoed behind him, and Sciro said, "Leave her alone, Brenton. She's not interested in being flambé."

Brenton growled, swinging around to face Sciro. "Think you can take me, little vampire?"

"For fuck's sake." Sciro said with a note of exasperation in his voice. "It's a library, not a boxing ring."

The other shifter grumbled, but he departed without saying anything else.

Sciro grinned at me. His frame was slimmer and he seemed more at home here in the library than Brenton, but when he smiled a little shiver ran through my gut. Shifter guys only seemed to come in one brand: sexy as hell.

"I didn't need saving," I said, unable to help an answering smile.

He licked a fang. "I know, but it gave me an excuse to come over here." His eyes ran over the books on the table, and his grin slipped. "You interested in spirit shifters?"

I swallowed. "I just don't know anything about them. And the Professors never say anything in class."

Sciro shrugged. "They're banned by the Council, you know. Killed at birth."

"They're unstable, and they tend to go mad." I gestured to the books. "They told me that."

His lips tightened.

"But they didn't tell me exactly what they are. What form do they take?"

"All forms," he said. "They can be any earth, air, fire, or water forms."

My shoulders stiffened. Last night's dreams of splashing in the ocean ran through my mind. My phase was shifting. "All of them?"

He nodded. "And spirit forms, like the kitsune and even—" He took a ragged breath as if remembering something. "A kind of pure spirit form."

A knot tightened in my stomach. Was this what my dreams meant? Forcing my voice to stay casual, I asked, "They always go crazy? There hasn't been a spirit shifter that was somehow okay?"

"They all go mad." He frowned at me, dark eyebrows pinching. "Why are you asking?"

I smiled unsteadily. "The books. They make such amazing art. It's so sad to lose that from the world."

"That's true," he said, studying my face. "It is a loss. But—" His mouth pressed into a thin line. "The attacks from Kaiden Hartsman are proof enough of what a risk an uncontrolled spirit shifter is to our world."

Intertwining my fingers, I said, "Yeah, I heard about Monica's dad."

"Not just him," Sciro said fiercely. "Seven shifters were killed in the attacks. They might not have been so high-ranking, but they were still our people."

My stomach soured. People were injured and dead because of a spirit shifter. Was I one too? All those dreams had to mean that I was, didn't they? I could already feel my phase shifting—water was next—and soon

I'd turn eighteen. After that, I would shift. What would I shift into?

"Spirit shifters are bad news, Hailey," he said softly. "Stay away from them."

I nodded. "Thanks. There's just so much about this world that I don't know."

"You'll get there," he said.

I started putting away my books, trying to keep my hands from trembling. Sciro turned to go, and I let him walk away.

This was something I needed to figure out on my own. I was a spirit shifter. A deranged killer. How long did I have left? Would I go crazy as soon as I shifted? Or later?

I squeezed my hands together. Would they know what I was? My breath hitched. Sciro had said he couldn't tell by looking at me, but once I shifted, would it be clear? Or would they notice my dreams as Mr. Reed had? My heart beat sped up.

They were going to execute me as soon as they found out. I shoved the books back on the shelf, and grabbed my bag. How long could I hide what I was? I needed to get away from the school. Maybe if I was away from everyone, I wouldn't hurt anyone.

Pushing open the library door, I headed down the dark hall. It was late, and the passage was quiet. The tears that had threatened burst forth. I was going to hurt Sciro and Terrin and Adrian. I wouldn't be able to control myself.

All the stories that I'd read tonight about the murderous spirit shifters ran through my mind. I was evil, and I hadn't even known it.

15

Adrian

Head down, I plowed across the courtyard. I'd taken to going to the pool late at night to avoid Monica. She seemed to think we had something together because both our parents were on the Council and we'd played together as kids. Well, that and the few rolls in the hay we'd enjoyed. But I slept with a lot of girls. It never meant anything, and Monica should have known that. I'd made my intentions perfectly clear.

After last term, I had thought that I'd finally gotten her to back off. I sighed. Then her dad had been hurt and I'd comforted her. Now she thought we were a couple. If it had been my parent to be injured, I'd have been equally upset. I couldn't seem to convince her that our parents having similar jobs, and similar dangers, didn't make us fated lovers.

Still, the pools were quiet at this time. Most of the other water shifters seemed to use them during the day. The halls were peaceful. Almost everyone had retired to their dorms. Relief trickled through me.

I headed into the stairwell and nearly crashed into Hailey, tears streaming down her face. My hands reflexively grasped her shoulders. "What's wrong?"

She shook her head, unable or unwilling to tell me.

Girls in tears didn't scare me. I guess that's one of the reasons they all liked me so much. I was willing to listen. Sliding my arm across Hailey's shoulders, I turned her to the stairs leading downward. "I'm going for a swim. Why don't you come along?"

"I don't know how to swim," she said, hiccuping.

Waggling my eyebrows, I grinned. "I'm a very good teacher."

The corner of her mouth quirked, and she rubbed the back of her hand across her eyes. Hailey took a breath, and met my gaze, her dark green eyes wet. Then, she bit her lip and nodded.

I led her down the steps and into the dark caverns. The rocky outcropping that the school was built on had a cave system, but the builders had enhanced them, adding lighting and warm salt-water pools. They'd made the necessary wiring and additions as unobtrusive as possible so the caverns felt natural.

We slipped through three or four rooms before I found the pool I liked the best. It was smaller than some of the others, but it had rock formations that served as seats in the shallower end. I stripped efficiently and dove into the water. The feel of the water across my skin was like the caress of a lover. When I crested the surface again, I sighed in contentment.

Glancing back at Hailey, I found her standing at the edge, arms wrapped across her chest and her eyes wide. "Come on in. The water's fine."

"You're naked," she whispered, her voice echoing anyway.

I chuckled. "Yeah, clothes just slow me down." I swam closer to her. "You can leave your underwear on if it makes you more comfortable."

A blush stained her cheeks a pretty rose color. Was she really an innocent? It was unusual for a shifter to not partake in sexual activity, especially before we could shift. Human hormones had nothing on a trapped form.

She took off her shoes and socks and sat on the edge of the water.

Sliding her legs and feet into the water, she gasped. Her plaid skirt slid up her thighs, exposing their tender skin.

It was the hottest thing I'd ever seen. I swallowed, willing my cock not to harden. That would only frighten her more. Closing my eyes, I took deep breaths trying to focus on a word like Professor Frank had explained.

Control. Control. Control. Don't scare the hot chick. Forcing a Sciro-like academic tone into my voice, I said, "They use heaters to keep the water temperature even."

"Oh," she said softly. Her internal argument was written all over her face. She didn't know me well enough to get naked and thought I must be trying to seduce her. This was some kind of trick.

It stung that she couldn't trust me, but I shoved down my irritation. I had a feeling she didn't trust anyone. What had they done to her before she'd come here? It was odd enough for someone to start Thornbriar so late, but she'd come in like a dog waiting to be kicked. I grimaced. Not that Greta and Monica had resisted throwing the first strike.

Watching her struggle, I thought for sure she was going to let modesty win.

But then her eyes flashed and she yanked her white top over her head, exposing her white lace bra. It was a standard one, no frills, but her perfectly formed mounds made my cock harden anyway. She stood, slipping off her skirt.

Her eyes darted over to me, and her blush deepened, but then she said a barely audible, "Fuck it." The granny undies and the bra followed her clothes, and she dived into the pool as gracefully as if she'd been doing it her whole life.

She came up sputtering though. I hurried over and slid my arm under her shoulders, keeping her afloat.

With a shy smile, she said, "Thank you."

I stared at her, stunned. *Damn.* I was starting to think that I'd never met a more dangerous female.

"So, how do I do this?"

Pulling myself together, I set to the business of teaching her to swim. Not that it was hard. She was a natural. Her strokes through the water were so smooth, and her form was perfect. If I hadn't known better, I'd have thought she was a water shifter. We get so much practice swimming in our dreams that it comes to us easily, even without formal training.

But that was ridiculous. Sciro had said she was an earth shifter.

"You're good at this," I said, holding her up with one hand on the smooth skin of her stomach.

"Thanks." She didn't look back, but the muscles of her back tightened.

I frowned. She knew something that she wasn't telling me. Hadn't I proven my trustworthiness?

Had someone said something about me? Even though I dated around, I was always honest. I wasn't looking for a long-term commitment. I just wanted to have fun, and the girls knew that. But here I hadn't even made a pass at this chick and she was acting like I was a jerk who couldn't be trusted.

Maybe she was the one being dishonest. Worth a shot. I leaned down close to her ear and whispered, "I know something about secrets."

A fierceness crept into her voice. "I don't know what you are talking about."

I crowed internally. My mother would be so proud. Her place on the Council depended on her ability to read people, and Hailey was broadcasting loud and clear. "As well as being a good teacher, I'm a good listener."

Hailey shook her head.

Smiling, I let it pass this time. "I'm going to let go. Swim to the side."

"I can't," she said with a gulp.

"I'm sure you can." I released my hand but stayed nearby in case I'd been wrong. I was rarely wrong, though.

She sank a bit, but then her feet moved faster and she propelled herself to the edge. Her hand closed over the smooth rocks, and she looked back at me, grinning. "I did it."

"Like I said—" I paused, watching the odd fear leap into her eyes. "I'm a good teacher."

"Yeah," she said with a chuckle.

I swam over to her. "Shall we meet again tomorrow night? Same time, same place?"

A blush heated her cheeks as if she had just remembered we were naked in the pool together. "Sounds good."

Props for that. She hadn't stammered at all, despite her embarrassment. Hailey was such a weird mixture of innocent and fierce. One minute she was blushing and the next, she was growling at me. This was a girl I could fall for. Good thing she was Terrin's and off-limits.

16

Hailey

"Choose a partner," Professor Alexander announced as he passed out the worksheets. "There are limited microscopes, and you will all need to share."

I glanced around. Even though I'd been here a couple of weeks, I still didn't know anyone well enough to partner. Looking toward Terrin, I found he was still avoiding me. I swallowed.

"Brenton," the professor said. "You team up with Hailey."

Hell no. Brenton looked about as excited about the idea as I was. He huffed and stomped over to my table. In the science lab, the high tables required bar stools to reach them. Perched on one, I crossed my arms and glared at Brenton.

"Careful there, Rosie Posie," he said. "Don't want to Humpty Dumpty it."

I groaned. "Professor, I need a different partner."

The professor glanced over at us and shook his head irritably. "Now, class, the first slide we are looking at today is of an onion."

"Guess you're stuck with me, Rosie." Brenton began laying out the slides in order along the middle of the table. He flicked on the microscope and peered in, adjusting the controls.

"My name's Hailey."

He shrugged. "I don't really care."

Flipping my hair back, I hopped off my stool. "Let me have a look."

Brenton continued to look and write on his sheet, ignoring me.

I shoved him, or at least I tried to shove him, but he was so big and muscled that it was like pushing a rock wall.

He flinched away from me as if I had burned him, then raised his head, eyes blazing. "Don't touch me."

"Then let me have a turn," I said, hands on my hips. Stepping forward, I ignored him and peered into the microscope. Adjusting the dials to clarify the image, I wrote some notes on my sheet. I could hear his breathing behind me as he tried to bring himself under control. What was wrong with him? "Can you hand me the next slide?"

"No."

I lifted my head and studied him. Guess I might as well ask. He couldn't hate me any more than he already did. "What's your problem?"

"None of your damn business, Rosie," he growled. "Now finish up. It's my turn."

With a shrug, I stepped aside. My arm accidentally brushed his, and he winced. I frowned. It wasn't like we had loads of space, and we only had one microscope. He acted like I had the freaking plague. This was going to be a long project.

At the end of class, Professor Alexander said, "Leave the materials on your tables. We'll continue tomorrow."

"How long are we working with slides, Professor?" Brenton asked, his tone moderate.

So, he could be polite when he wanted to.

The professor smiled. "All week."

Oh, hell.

17

Hailey

After swimming every night that week with Adrian, I slept so deeply that I didn't remember dreaming at all. Had swimming alleviated my need to dream about the water? It was worth pondering. Professor Frank had said physical activity helped to control the shifter and relieved some of the agitation. Maybe I could stay hidden, stay alive a little longer.

I hadn't even noticed the nakedness after a while. At first it was all I could think of, the blush rising in my cheeks. As he started showing me the strokes, he was so gentle and careful that I stopped paying attention to the feel of bare skin.

Pulling on my school uniform, I grimaced. I'd meant to get some jeans and tee shirts, but I had no idea how. Were there trips into town for shopping? And might that be a good time to slip away? I ran a quick brush through my hair and headed down the stairs.

My stomach growled as I crossed the courtyard. Adrian leaned against a tree; his eyes half-closed. His blond hair was tousled as if he'd barely run a comb through it. I started toward him, to thank him for last night, when Monica rushed by me.

"Adrian," she called in a sing-song voice.

I rolled my eyes.

"She's always like that," Terrin said beside me. "She thinks they're fated to be together."

Turning toward him, I raised an eyebrow. "Are you talking to me now?"

"Hey, I'm sorry." He scratched his neck. "I got a little spooked."

"Spooked?"

"Monica's dad getting hurt..." He frowned. "It brought up some old issues for me about the safety of those I care about."

"Care about?" I blinked at him. We barely knew each other and he was already worried about caring too much?

"Yeah, um." He scratched the long scar on his arm. It crisscrossed the muscle like a knife wound. "But I'd like to be . . . friends, if you'll allow it?"

He pushed all my buttons: gentle and caring one minute, cold and aloof the next. How could I ever trust him? But I wanted to. I'd felt connected to him since the first moment I met him. Everything about Terrin pulled me in. His skin glowed golden brown in the cool morning sunlight, and his topaz eyes watched me, waiting. It was my call, he seemed to say. "Okay," I said softly. "Let's try."

He smiled and jerked his head toward the dining room doors. "Wanna grab something to eat?"

"Yes, I'd like that."

We headed into the dining hall, and the aroma of bacon, eggs, and hash browns greeted my nose. My mouth watered at just the smell.

Terrin guided me to the line with a hand at the small of my back. It should have been too intimate a gesture, but with Terrin it felt right. I don't know what it was about him, but he could do things that I'd have smacked anyone else for even trying.

At the end of the line, I glanced around the packed cafeteria and wondered if I should go back to my room anyway.

"My place?" he asked roughly.

I glanced at him and grinned at the lines of strain around his eyes. He really was trying not to let whatever happened in his past get to him. "How about we just go out in the courtyard?"

He nodded. We wandered back into the quad and found a spot near Adrian. Monica was still all over him, and Adrian glanced over at us, his eyes pleading.

Terrin snorted, then said, "Hey Monica."

"What?" she asked, looking up at him. She shot me a nasty glare.

"I heard Greta asking for you in the dining hall." He sighed. "Some kind of girl emergency."

Monica jumped to her feet and ran into the hall.

Adrian breathed a heavy sigh of relief. "Thanks, buddy."

"You can say no, you know." Terrin said, dropping down into the grass.

"Have you tried saying no to Monica Gray?" Adrian asked.

"No need," Terrin said. "She's not interested in any of us lower beings."

I giggled. They both glanced at me and then broke into laughter themselves.

We dug into our meals, enjoying the cool morning.

After breakfast, we headed into class. Professor Frank's was the first of the day. She had yoga mats laid out along the gym floor, and she asked us to sit in pairs facing each other. Terrin sat across from me, and Adrian shrugged, wandering off to find his own partner.

Professor Frank clapped her hands at the front of the class. "Now take a deep breath from your diaphragm, everyone, and let it go. And again."

The breathing exercises had become familiar in the last week. Which was good. Professor Frank said they were the basis of expert control, and I needed that if I was going to hide the fact that I was a spirit shifter for even one more year.

"Okay, turn around, and sit back-to-back with your partner," Professor Frank said.

I arched an eyebrow at Terrin and he smiled. We spun and did as she asked, sitting in lotus position with our backs against each other.

His back was muscular and warm against mine. My heart thudded against my chest, echoing in my ears.

"Lay your palm against your chest," Professor Frank said. "Notice your breathing and the breathing of your partner. Don't try to sync them, just notice."

Closing my eyes, I forced myself to take slow, easy breaths as we'd been taught. Terrin's back moved with his breaths and despite our instructions, we moved into rhythm. We were so connected, and I didn't understand why.

Terrin lay his free hand on top of mine, our fingers automatically interlacing. My breath stuttered, but I steadied it. *Stay the course.*

My eyes opened and I caught sight of Adrian and his partner behind me. His lips turned down as if he were sad, but once he realized I was watching him, he gave me a wink. I shook my head. At least he hadn't had to partner with the dreaded Monica this time.

We finished our breathing exercises and stood up. Terrin still held my fingers as he turned and searched my face. His dark eyebrows furled as if he was trying to understand. I didn't understand what this was between us either. Did shifters just feel things stronger than humans? Or did we have some special connection? I gave him a shrug, and he smiled, releasing my hand.

Professor Frank led us through a series of yoga poses. I tried to breathe and be in the moment.

18

Terrin

My jaguar stretched and purred like a housecat as we went through the yoga poses. He knew that Hailey was the one for us, and he was just waiting for my pesky human side to come around. We were safe at school. I shouldn't worry about protecting her from more than mean girls and that asshole Brenton.

Still, I worried. Even as I wrapped her fingers in mine and we breathed in unison, I was troubled. I didn't really know anything about this girl, except my instincts told me she was mine. Even my pack mates seemed a little leery of her. Sciro had been reluctant to just walk her to the library. What did that mean about their instincts? I trusted my brothers more than myself most days.

"You alright, man?" asked Adrian as we gathered up our mats.

I nodded. "Girl troubles."

He laughed.

My brother didn't have troubles with women. He always knew exactly how to handle them, whether they were laughing or crying. That's what made watching him with Monica so amusing. She refused to be deterred by his nonchalance. Monica had already made her mind up about what they should be, and she wouldn't take no for an answer.

"Not that you'd know anything about that," I said with a smirk.

He snorted. "No, nothing at all."

"Just a little Moni-stalker." I chuckled.

Adrian laughed even harder, holding his side and trying to catch his breath.

"What's going on?" Hailey asked behind us.

We both looked at her and then at each other, and tried to rein ourselves in. Adrian wiped tears from his eyes, and I leaned against the stacked yoga mats.

Hailey looked offended, her shoulders bunching and her eyes narrowing.

"It's not—" I shook my head, catching my breath. "Not about you."

She still looked puzzled but allowed me to take her mat and put it on the stack.

"Come on," Adrian said with a waggle of his eyebrows. "Let's get out of here before Monica catches us."

Hailey grinned.

19

Hailey

Terrin and Adrian strolled with me across the courtyard. I had Tutoring Assistance next, and they both had other classes to get to, but it was nice to have a few minutes to walk together. Terrin took my hand, and I let him. His flips back and forth were confusing, but I was beginning to think he might mean it this time.

I shivered as a cold wind whipped through me. The weather had turned again, and the leaves were changing colors on the trees. I'd have to dig out some of the school sweaters from the closet. I grimaced as goose-bumps rose on my skin.

"You're cold," Terrin said.

"Yeah, a bit," I said with a small smile. "I'd better find some cold weather clothes."

He nodded, pulling me closer to him to share his warmth. Adrian noticed and moved closer on my other side, blocking the wind.

Warmth uncurled in my gut. Before I'd come here, I'd never imagined hanging out with two gorgeous guys so concerned for my welfare. To be honest, anyone paying attention to me felt strange.

Despite their closeness, another cold breeze blasted through me and I quivered. At Hasting's House, I'd have given anything for clothes that weren't shabby dresses, but these school uniforms weren't much better. Humph. "I'd like to get some clothes. Monica said I had some kind of stipend?"

"Yeah," Adrian said. "It should be plenty for you to shop."

"Um . . . where do I go? Is there a bus to the stores?" I hadn't been to a real store since I was a little girl. What was it like?

Terrin squeezed his arm around my waist. "The nearest town is pretty far. There won't be a bus trip until closer to the holidays."

"Oh."

"But," Adrian said. "You can shop online."

"I can?" I winced. Just another thing I was dumb about. I'd seen people on TV use computers, but I'd never been near one myself.

A troubled frown creased Terrin's forehead. "Have you ever used the internet?"

I shook my head.

Terrin squeezed me again. "We can help. Meet at our suite during lunch?"

Adrian nodded. "We'll bring the food and show you the ropes."

"Okay," I said hesitantly. "Thank you."

They grinned at me as if I'd made their day by asking them for something.

I swallowed. I didn't like being so needy. Learning to fend for myself in the outside world was a must, though.

When we reached the building, I unwound myself from Terrin's arms. "I've got T.A."

Terrin's eyes followed me. "See you soon."

I smiled and turned toward the stairwell. I felt both of their eyes on me as I headed up the stairs. My gut swirled. I knew I could only count on myself. Why was I trusting these guys? Because there was so much I didn't know and they could help me. I bit my lip. But was I just putting them in danger? I was a banned shifter, hiding out, and I was dangerous.

"Hailey?" a male voice asked.

In my distraction, I'd been gazing at my feet and almost ploughed into my recruiter. "Mr. Reed, how are you?"

He smiled. "I'm good. How are you settling in?"

I opened my mouth and closed it again. Hadn't the guys said it was weird for Mr. Reed to hang around so long? Was he suspicious of me? Or was he just worried because he knew where I'd come from? I forced a smile. "I'm doing fine."

"No more thoughts of running away?" he inquired gently.

My fear must have shown on my face because he continued, "When I was a young wolf, I, also, wanted to revel in my freedom."

I grimaced. "Not much freedom here."

He raised a burly eyebrow. "But more than where you came from."

With a sigh, I nodded.

"And even greater freedom awaits if you can gain control," he said, gesturing for me to walk with him toward the library.

"I suppose." If they didn't discover what I really was and execute me for being a spirit shifter before I did.

"The impatience of youth." He chuckled.

At the library door, he stopped and turned toward me. His face darkened, and his eyes searched mine. "I don't know why Kaiden Hartsman was looking for you that night."

My heart skipped a beat.

"But," Mr. Reed continued. "I know he is not a man who easily gives up." He reached out and took my hands in his. "If you were to leave Thornbriar, it would not only be ill-advised, it may be dangerous. He may still be looking."

A dangerous spirit shifter was looking for me? My hands would have trembled if they hadn't been in Mr. Reed's firm grasp. "What would he want with me? I'm not on the Council or anything."

"I don't know." He exhaled. "But he has shown an unusual interest and I fear for your safety. Promise me you'll stay put?"

"I will," I said. *For as long as I can*, I added silently. As much as I didn't want to get in the bad guy's cross-hairs, I'd rather risk that than certain death here if they discovered my true element.

He didn't quite believe me, but he let my hands go. "Off to class with you."

"Thanks, Mr. Reed," I said, and I meant it. I hadn't wanted to be rescued, but I was glad to be here all the same. I was learning things about myself I might not have anywhere else. But I was also terrified for whole new reasons.

"You're welcome, Hailey." He turned and headed back down the passage.

After I finished my Tutoring Assistance, I headed down to the boys' suite. I knocked.

Adrian opened the door. His golden hair lay in wet curls against his head, as if he had just gotten out of the shower. He wore jeans slung low across his hips, and his smooth muscled chest just made me want to reach out and stroke him. I shook myself. What was wrong with me?

"Come in," he said. "Terrin's gone down to fetch us some grub."

"Okay," I said, heat rising in my cheeks. When had I started blushing over every little thing? I'd seen him naked before. Why was the wet hair and chest even bothering me? I dropped down on the couch, squeezing my legs together.

He rubbed his towel across his hair, only mussing it further, and draped it over his shoulders. Then he leaned down and grabbed a drink from the fridge. "You want a soda?"

"Sure."

After popping the drink tab, he set it down on the edge of the table and then plopped down next to me. My heart beat faster with him nearby, and I took a casual sip of the drink. Bubbles ran down my throat, and I tried to ignore the warmth of the body next to me.

Adrian picked up a tablet from among the mess of the coffee table. "Might as well get started," he said with a shrug. "You'll have a tablet in your room too. It's standard issue for the students."

"Oh. I guess Monica would have told me about it if I hadn't pissed her off."

He gave me a gentle smile. "You should try to talk to her. Monica's not that bad."

I raised an eyebrow. "I thought you were avoiding her."

Adrian shrugged. "Monica and I have been friends since we were little. Our parents often worked late on Council business, and we would find ourselves stuck together with nothing to do."

I nodded, leaning forward for the story.

"There was this one time I thought it'd be great fun to slide down the banisters like we were in some movie." He chuckled. "We did it several times successfully, and then Monica missed a turn and slammed into the wall. She broke her leg."

His eyes drifted up. "I had to call the ambulance and wait with her until it came. Our parents didn't even notice we were gone until later that night." He grimaced. "Typical in my case, but her dad's not usually so forgetful."

My heart squeezed, and I lay a hand on his arm.

His face softened. "We are good friends, or at least we were until she decided that we should be lovers."

"You slept with her?" I asked.

"I'm a bit of a ladies' man, if you hadn't heard." He shrugged guiltily. "I'm not likely to turn down an advance."

"But your friendship was ruined," I said.

"Not entirely, but she's been dogged in her pursuit of me ever since." He ran a hand through his hair. "I keep telling her that if we'd been fated, there'd have been a mate tattoo, but she's not listening."

"A mate tattoo?"

He smiled. "I keep forgetting how new you are to our world. When a fated couple makes love for the first time, a tattoo appears on their upper arms." He gestured right around his shoulder. "Vibrant green vines and leaves."

"The same tattoo?" I stared at his arms, but there wasn't even a hint of color.

"Yes and no," he said. "Everyone gets vines and leaves, but as their relationship grows so does the tattoo."

"Grows?"

He gestured down his arm toward his wrist. "Intertwined in the leaves are symbols of the events in their relationship - a romantic getaway, new house, a child, and so on."

I frowned. "Doesn't Professor Ward have something like that? But his are faded?"

"Yes, his mate died." Adrian said.

"Oh."

"Often when half the couple dies, the other half wastes away, unable to live with the loss. Professor Ward is a very strong shifter indeed to have survived it."

"Will he mate again?"

Adrian shook his head. "Shifter mates are for life. One could love again, but I've never heard of anyone mating a second time."

20

Hailey

I 'd been confronted with so many new ideas since I'd come to Thornbriar, but fated mates was the most intense. Imagine making such a bond with someone just because of a sexual encounter. What if they didn't know each other well? If they'd just been hooking up? So many questions ran through my head. The tattoo marked someone, and it didn't seem like they had any choice in the matter. Wouldn't they feel confined, even if they loved the other shifter? "Sounds like a trap," I mused.

Adrian laughed. "Not really. Even if a fated couple isn't in love yet, they will be. The tattoo just marks something they already know."

"But then you're tied to this one person for life."

He waggled his eyebrows. "That's why I like to keep my options open."

"But any time you sleep with someone, she could be the one and the tattoo would appear." I tilted my head. "Isn't that a risk?"

"I guess." He grinned. "She'd just have to reform me from my rakish ways."

"Assuming you could be reformed," I said with a snort.

There was a knock at the door, and Adrian stood and crossed to it. "We'd better get to looking for clothes," he said as he swung the door open. He probably assumed it was Terrin, trying to carry three plates, but Monica stood there.

She stared at his shirtless chest and me sitting on the couch, and her mouth gaped. With a gasp, she exclaimed, "You told me she was Terrin's girl."

"We were just . . ." Adrian's voice trailed off at her furious expression.

With a huff, Monica turned and fled down the corridor. She nearly knocked over Terrin. He had to jump to the side to avoid her, the plates rattling in his hands. "Some friends you have," she muttered.

"What's her problem?" Terrin asked.

Adrian shrugged and grabbed a plate to help him inside.

Today, the menu was macaroni and cheese with roasted chicken and steamed vegetables. The scents mingled in the air, and I took a big whiff. I might not be in wolf phase anymore, but I still appreciated a good meal. After my early experiences, I probably always would. Holding the warm plate in my lap, I sighed in pleasure.

Sitting down next to me, Terrin grinned. "I love a girl who can eat."

Adrian pulled a black tee shirt on and plopped down on my other side. He flicked on the tablet and said, "Might as well get started."

I swallowed a bite, nodding and staring at the screen.

He pulled up what he called a browser, showing me the icon first and then he flipped through a few stores. I appreciated his patience and his clear explanations.

I wasn't a complete idiot, and I had seen some of these things before, at least on television that I watched with the girls. My memories of my life before Hastings House were hazy, but I was sure I must have played with tablets and phones.

"You can search most anything and find some information on it," Terrin said. "But I wouldn't recommend searching shifters."

"Why not?"

They laughed.

Leaning back against the couch, Terrin said, "The information isn't very accurate. At best, you'll get fairy tales."

"Or porn," Adrian said.

"Oh." The heat rose in my cheeks again, and I steeled myself. I refused to be a blushing maiden, even if in fact, the words were true.

Adrian stopped at a clothing website. "This one's good. What are you looking for?"

"Jeans, tee shirts," I said. "And a coat." I shivered and Terrin's leg shifted closer, offering me his warmth.

Adrian clicked on the images and after my approving nod, set about putting several pairs of jeans and shirts in the cart.

I frowned. "How do you know my size?"

"Um . . ." He glanced at me and then at Terrin, who bristled beside me. "Girl experience."

Relaxing, Terrin chuckled. "Of course."

I had questions about that, but Adrian didn't seem to want to talk about it in front of his friend. Terrin and I had been getting closer. I enjoyed his company, but I didn't like the idea that they all saw me as his property. We hadn't made any commitments. We hadn't even been on a real date, and the other guys walked on eggshells when he was around.

Adrian showed me a few coats, and I picked out a black leather one with a fake fur collar. The guys shuddered at the real fur ones. I guess knowing people who turned furry made pelts less attractive.

The cart was full, and Terrin asked for my school debit card.

"What?"

Adrian grimaced. "Guess that's another thing Monica didn't get around to telling you."

Terrin explained that the school put my scholarship stipend on a card, like a credit card, and I could use it to shop. "I'll cover it this time."

"No, I'll go get it from my room, now that I know what I'm looking for," I said, standing.

He clicked in the info and said, "No worries. It's all done. You should get the items within a day or two."

"Thank you," I said, twisting my fingers in my hair. I didn't like being indebted to him, but he hadn't given me much choice. Still, it was exciting to think of getting the items so soon. "Do they come all the way up here?"

Adrian frowned as if he sensed my unease. "No, they are delivered to the airfield. Here's the address, for next time." He handed me a paper where he'd jotted it down. "The school flies them up here, and the staff delivers it to your room."

"Okay. Thank you both." I bounced from foot to foot.

Terrin stood and took my hands, stilling me. "It's okay, Hailey. Let me walk you to class."

I gazed into his topaz eyes, and butterflies swirled in my gut. What was I doing? Running from the one good thing life had dropped in my lap. Terrin had been nothing but kind to me, and I acted like he was forcing me into a cage. My nerves skittered under my skin, and I bounced again. "I don't think I can go to class."

He studied me and nodded. "Let's go for a run."

"Yes," I said with a smile.

When we got down the steps and out into the back yard, the cold wind cut through me. I hesitated at the doorway, staring at the dark forests at the end of the yard.

"Come on," Terrin said, grabbing my hand and pulling me out.

"It's cold," I protested.

He pulled his sweatshirt over his head and handed it to me.

I pulled it on, smelling his sweet forest scent. I followed him down the trodden path into the woods. The sun peeked through the trees and I breathed in the fresh air. This wasn't city air or even the stale air inside the campus buildings. This was freedom.

Terrin took off running between the pine trees.

Laughing, I followed. I wasn't as fast as I would have been during a wolf phase, but he wasn't trying to outpace me.

He circled back and whispered, "Run." Then he took off again.

I ran as fast as I could. The movement heated my still bare legs, and the sweatshirt covered my fingers. We went beyond the circle of the academy, climbing higher onto the mountain. Somewhere beyond us was the fence and its electric boundary, but I pushed those thoughts away. Thornbriar had acres of woods within its borders. We could run for miles, and we did.

When the woods opened into a grassy meadow, Terrin reached out and grabbed me. We tumbled to the ground, our bodies pressed together and our breath coming in harsh pants. His eyes met mine, and we grinned at each other. This had been what I'd needed to stop being bound up in all my worries. Freedom, to run and not to think. Freedom to just be.

Our breath mingled in the cool air, but I didn't feel cold. His topaz eyes glowed. My eyes drifted to his lips, and I licked mine, thinking about another kind of release. I was free to choose who to be with and when, in a way I hadn't ever been able to before.

He asked permission and, at my nod, brought his mouth down on mine. A different kind of warmth uncurled in my gut. I wrapped my arms around his back, curling my fingers in his dark hair, and kissed him back.

I'd been worried about him staking his claim on me, but out here in the wild, I didn't feel trapped. I felt liberated. Free enough to make my own claim as I raked my fingers down his back.

Terrin moaned against my mouth, his hands trailing down my body. I moved against him, feeling the hard length of him against my core. Fire roared through me, and I wasn't cold any longer.

His fingers slipped under the hem of his sweatshirt, yanking it off me and then unbuttoning my standard-issue white school shirt. He stroked my nipple through the bra and I arched against him, gasping.

Everywhere his hands went, he left a trial of fire. Sliding his hand behind my back, he flicked open the latch on my bra and sent quivers through my skin. He pushed the bra up and cupped my breast in his hand. Then he leaned down and sucked on the pebbled nipple.

My thoughts fled as sensation raced through me. Even when I'd been naked with Adrian the other night, he hadn't touched me so intimately. Terrin's touch made me feel alive in a way I'd never experienced. I reached out, trying to touch him in the way that he touched me, but I floundered. I'd never done anything like this before.

Terrin paused his ministrations, and grasped my hand. "Hailey," he asked softly. "Are you a virgin?"

I swallowed. "Yes."

"I'm sorry," he said. "You probably don't want your first time to be laying on the cold ground."

What was I supposed to say to that? I wanted to kiss him. I chose this. Yet, now, as he moved away, I shivered uncontrollably.

Terrin rebuttoned my blouse, and pulled his sweat shirt back over my head.

"I didn't want to stop," I said, brushing my hair back from my face.

He smiled and cupped my chin. "I know. But I care too much about you to rush your first time. Let's take it slow."

I blinked. He genuinely cared about my experience. It'd been too many years since anyone had been concerned about me and how I felt. "Thank you."

Stroking his finger along the side of my face, he said, "I've never known anyone like you, Hailey. I've wanted you since the moment I laid eyes on you. But I think we have something real here, and I'd like to take our time."

"Okay," I said, running my teeth over my lip. It wouldn't help my escape plans if we made love and mate-bonded. I didn't even know where the thought had come from, but I knew it was right. This was a guy I could spend the rest of my life with, and if I was caught, he'd be devastated. As strong as Terrin was, I couldn't imagine him carrying on with a faded mate tattoo after they killed me.

"Dark thoughts," he said, tracing my brow.

I shook myself and grinned. I knew because Sciro had told me, but I wanted Terrin to tell me himself. "Have you shifted yet?"

"Yes." He crossed his arms in front of his chest. "Why?"

Sitting up, I exclaimed, "Show me!"

He raised an eyebrow. "I repeat, why?"

"I've never seen anyone shift before. Don't you think I should see it before I experience it?"

Terrin laughed. "All right. All right."

I watched him stand and shed his clothes. While both he and Adrian were lean with compact muscles all over their bodies, Adrian's skin had been a pale cream, almost hairless. Terrin's richer ochre skin had thick patches of brown-black hair under his arms and between his legs. Terrin's chest was broader than Adrian's with thick cords of muscles across his stomach. My breath caught in my throat as he flexed. "Does it hurt?"

"What?"

Blinking, I stared at his flaccid member and then blurted, "The shift. Does the shift hurt?"

"It can." His lips twisted in memory. "If uncontrolled. That's why we spend so much time practicing focus."

I nodded.

"And physical activity helps too. The guys and I go for a run almost every night, and we hit the gym as often as we can."

"I see." A blush threatened to rise in my cheeks, but I shoved it down.

He grinned and then closed his eyes. The forest seemed to quiet around us, the small birds and animals tucking into their homes as if they knew a predator was coming. He arched his back, his mouth widened, and the change rippled over him, from head to toe. I didn't dare blink, afraid I would miss the soundless process. A black jaguar, his hair black but with lighter spots along his flank, paced before me.

"Terrin?" I held out my hand. We hadn't talked about whether he could still hear and understand me in animal form. I guessed he could though, because the big cat paced forward and rubbed its face against my hand. His eyes were still Terrin's eyes, their topaz even brighter against the black coat. Leaning forward, I stroked his soft fur. I buried my face in it, breathing in Terrin's unmistakable forest scent. "You're amazing."

He huffed against my ear, and I grinned.

21

Hailey

I'd almost forgotten that we'd missed our afternoon classes by the time we got back to campus. Only one more remained today, so Terrin and I held hands as we crossed the green and headed into our History class.

Professor Roth stood at the front of the room in her usual stylish dress, a deep navy blue today. On her thin nose, black-rimmed spectacles perched. She frowned at us for our tardiness, but I couldn't summon any guilt. Terrin and I slid into two seats near the back of class. I tried to focus on the Professor's words, but it was harder today than it usually was. I grinned, my thoughts full of our adventures in the woods.

Monica sat three rows ahead of me, and she peered back over her shoulder, her eyes full of venom. What had I . . . oh yeah, Adrian. Would she even believe me if I tried to explain? It was completely innocent.

"Isn't that right, Hailey?"

"Yes," I answered automatically, and the other students laughed.

The professor smiled. "Now that you've joined us back here on earth, we can perhaps continue our lesson?"

Heat filled my cheeks. Nodding, I picked up my pencil.

"The spirit shifter colony of 1920," Professor Roth said.

I raised my hand.

"Yes, Hailey?" she asked.

"Are there still spirit shifter colonies?"

"Indeed, there are small groups of rebels and refugees scattered around."

My brain whirled. "But how?"

"Well, although the Council has a law that spirit shifters are to be killed at birth, not everyone abides by this law."

I blinked. "Aren't they arrested?"

"If they are caught, yes, but some outlaw groups exist." The Professor sighed. "And by banding together, they have been able to resist the Council's efforts to enforce the law."

If I could get away from the academy, maybe I could escape execution by finding one of these groups. "Does the Council know where they are?"

"No," Monica said. "If my father knew where they were, he'd have them bombed."

Greta flipped back her blonde hair, and said in a stage whisper, "If he could afford a bomb."

The girls around her tittered, and Monica's face flamed.

Eyeing Monica, I wondered what she'd done to bring Greta's wrath down on herself. I thought they were best friends.

Professor Roth ignored the jibe and continued on with her lecture. I listened closer, wondering if the story of the 1920s colony would give me any clue to those existing today. I nibbled on my lip. This could be the way I survived, among my own kind. But what happened when the whole group went crazy? Did they have some way of forestalling it? Or of curing the madness? If there was a cure, wouldn't the Council have rescinded the kill order?

22

Terrin

The movie played on the big screen. Sciro leaned back in the armchair, and Adrian perched on the end of the couch. Hailey snuggled against my side, and my arm wrapped around her shoulders. It felt right with her there. My jaguar purred. After all we had shared in the last few days, things were finally coming together. She was where she should have been all the time.

Adrian got up from the end of the couch and headed over to the fridge. He called, "Anybody want anything?"

Hailey raised her arm and said, "A Coke."

"Kinda late for a soda," I said against the top of her head. I could feel her shoulders tighten underneath my arm. "But whatever you want."

"Yeah, a coke," she said.

Adrian brought over two drinks, popping the tops. He pressed one against Hailey's bare foot, and she squealed. Then they both giggled.

My eyes narrowed as I watched them. Monica had been going on and on about Adrian yesterday. He'd been half-naked in the suite the other day when Hailey had come over. My brother was always like that. I never thought anything of it, but Monica had been so worried. She really believed there was something going on between them. I'd said no way.

My brother wouldn't do me like that.

Adrian leaned back on the couch. Hailey put her feet on his lap, and he tickled her toes.

"Hey, quit it!" Hailey exclaimed, laughing and hitting him with a pillow.

It's just Adrian being Adrian, and I shouldn't make anything of it. Hailey and I were together. He knew that. I should have been glad my pack mate enjoyed my mate's company.

Whoa. Had I just thought mate? I could feel my cat's utter relaxation, like *you didn't know that, you idiot?* If it'd been a house cat, it'd have been licking its paw and laughing at me. I squeezed Hailey closer, and she snuggled me. *Mate.*

The credits rolled. Sciro clicked off the screen, and then he headed back into his bedroom.

Adrian jumped up and muttered something about a swim. He disappeared out the door.

I grinned at Hailey. "Guess they're giving us some alone time."

She raised an eyebrow. "Thought it was getting late?"

"Not too late for this," I said, leaning in for a kiss.

Hailey kissed me back, wrapping her arms around me. Her tongue darted into my mouth, and she set my nerve endings on fire. I hardened instantly and rubbed my hand across her breasts. Everything in me called out to claim this female, but I wanted to give her time. Time to get used to our world and to want me as much as I wanted her.

What if we made love and the mate mark appeared? I'd have to protect her, not just here at Thornbriar, but out in the world. And I had already proved that I couldn't protect the things I loved. At these thoughts, my passion cooled and I extricated myself from Hailey's embrace.

"I guess it is late. You should go," I said.

She frowned. "Did I do something wrong?"

"No," I said. "It's just me. More tired than I thought."

"Okay." She stood and walked toward the door.

Her new jeans clung to her perfect ass, and I groaned. My cat growled. I was not supposed to let this gorgeous thing walk away from us. I squeezed my hands into fists. We both needed time. She needed time to be ready for love-making, and I needed time to learn control. This really was the best solution as much as my cat hated it.

At the door, she glanced back, flipping her long hair over her shoulder. "Goodnight, Terrin."

I jumped up. "I should walk you back to your dorm."

She laughed. "It's just a few feet away."

Taking her hand, I led her down the hall and toward the stairs. "Come on."

23

Hailey

Terrin dropped me at my door with a sweet kiss. *Boy, can this guy kiss.* Energy hummed through my veins. He'd have been right, if I was going to bed, the soda would have been too much. But I wasn't going to bed. I gave him a few minutes to disappear down the corridor, then I took off for the pools.

I'd thrown a school sweater over my jeans and shirt to hold off the chill in the cool corridors. The halls were silent and dark. Not a soul seemed to be out of bed. It was a precious piece of silence in a busy day.

Ever since the day in the woods, Terrin had clung to my side like a barnacle. I loved the attention, and he was sexy as hell. Still, I couldn't stay at Thornbriar Academy forever. I needed to get out, and sooner rather than later. I hadn't shifted yet, but it could be any day now. I was still in my water phase, and if I did shift, I doubted it would be the expected wolf.

I needed a plan, but it all seemed hopeless. The fences were topped with electrical wires and deliveries were made by plane and truck. Even if I did escape, I'd be in acres and acres of forest. Sciro had said that spirit shifters could change into any form. Would that mean that, even if I was in a water form, I could choose to shift to wolf? There was just so much I didn't know.

Turning the corner, I breathed the warm salty air of the first cavern and sighed. This is what I needed. Every night that I went swimming, I avoided the water dreams. The element's needs were sated and the dreams unnecessary. One more way to avoid detection at the moment. My stomach swirled. Until I shifted and they killed me.

Adrian was already in the pool. His pale body cut across the water. I hurried over, stripping as I went, and dived in. Underwater, I opened my eyes, watching the reflecting lights make patterns on the bottom. No creatures lived in these pools, except a certain man-fish. I swam across the water, surfacing near the wall on the other side.

"You're getting good at this," Adrian said.

This routine had become an inside joke to us. I grinned. "All due to my excellent teacher."

He laughed, and lay his arms along the cold stone at the edge of the pool. Kicking his feet gently under the water, he watched me. "That movie sucked."

Giggling, I paddled over to him. "It wasn't that bad."

"Ha. You're just trying to take your boyfriend's side."

I shrugged my shoulders. "He isn't my boyfriend."

"You kiss, hold hands, and walk together . . ." He winked. "Seems like a boyfriend to me."

"He hasn't asked."

Adrian snorted. "He doesn't need to."

My brow furrowed. "Of course he does. I am not bought and paid for."

Running a hand through his blond hair, Adrian studied me. "Most girls would be thrilled to be on his arm."

"It's nice," I admitted. "But I don't belong to anyone but myself. And if Terrin wants a commitment, he needs to be upfront about it."

Adrian nodded. "I don't think he knows that. You might want to tell him."

"He might want to ask." I dove across the pool.

We swam in companionable silence for a few minutes.

Then Adrian stopped me, searching my face. "Where are you from, wild girl?" he asked.

"A very bad place," I said softly.

"Tell me."

"I was kidnapped when I was seven." I bit my lip. "Before that, I remember only blue skies, beaches, and my parents' arms."

His face stilled. "And then?"

"I was taken to Hastings House. They raised us to be sold for sex."

"Like cattle."

It wasn't often I saw Adrian serious. I wanted to stroke away the lines from his face. "It wasn't so bad really. I was fed, clothed, and cared for."

"Cared for?"

"Well, not in any sort of affectionate way. But if we followed the rules, kept our schedules, then they mostly ignored us."

"But you didn't follow the rules." He stroked the scar that lined the back of my shoulder. I'd almost forgotten it was there.

I snorted. "Of course not."

A grin spread across his face. "You're such a brave woman."

"Idiot, more like."

He grasped my shoulders and peered into my eyes. "No, Hailey. You need to own this. You fucking survived."

I stared back at him. "I fucking did."

And I would keep surviving. Even if it meant I had to leave the only place that had ever felt like home.

24

Sciro

The moon rose over the mountain as Terrin and I ran along the forest path. "So, you and Hailey are a thing?"

"Yup," he said.

"That's awesome, man."

"Yeah, I know. I still get scared though you know."

I nodded. We all had things in our pasts to keep us up at night. "Did she tell you about her life before?"

"Before? As in before Thornbriar?"

"Yeah."

He shook his head. "Not yet."

"Oh."

Pulling to a stop, he glared at me. "What's that supposed to mean?"

I shrugged. "It's just kinda a big thing to say she's your girlfriend and not know about her history."

"She tell you?"

Ducking my chin, I pushed a rock around with my toe. "Sorta."

"What the hell?" he growled. "First she's flirting with Adrian, and now she's telling you her secrets? What kind of girlfriend is she?"

Frowning, I asked, "Flirting with Adrian?"

"Yeah, Monica said . . ."

At least he had the common sense to looks sheepish. "You're believing Monica Fucking Gray when it comes to anything involving Adrian?"

He scratched his neck. "Shit, you're right man."

"Did you actually see them flirt?"

"I only saw that stuff during the movie night. You know, the tickling and stuff."

"Terrin, he's only treating her like a kid sister. That's probably the most appropriate way to treat your bro's mate."

He scuffed his feet on the grass. "Yeah, you're probably right."

"And I only know a little about her past because I asked. Have you asked her?"

"Well, no . . ."

Idiot. He was my pack brother, and I loved him, but sometimes he was so dense. Then it dawned on me. What if he hadn't really talked to her about any of this? "Terrin, man, you did ask her to be your girlfriend, didn't you?"

He blinked. "Well, I thought it was understood. I mean we've been holding hands and making out."

"Terrin, you have to make your wishes plain. Especially with a girl like Hailey."

Bristling, he frowned. "What's that supposed to mean?"

"Not my secrets to tell." I held my hands out, palms up. "But she's had a rough history."

"I figured that out. I met her trying to climb the fence to escape Thornbriar."

I grimaced. Sounded about right. After growing up where she did, I wouldn't expect Hailey to trust any place with a wall. "You need to talk to her. Not just kiss her."

He grunted. "Do you think there really is something going on between her and Adrian?"

"Hell no. Adrian wouldn't do that to you."

Nor would I. That's why I'd stayed as far away from Hailey as I could get. She was too much temptation. Just the smell of her in the common room after movie night had given me a hard-on for days. But she was Terrin's. We all knew that.

25

Hailey

I rolled over in my bed, the soft mattress giving beneath my weight. Today was my birthday. Hard to believe I'd already been at the school for a month. I stared at the morning light drifting through the curtained window. No one knew I was turning eighteen today. I didn't want them to start watching me for signs of a shift. I needed to get out of Thornbriar Academy before I shifted, and I still had no idea how.

Slipping out of bed, I dragged on some clothes. Tee shirts and jeans had almost completely replaced my school uniform. The scholarship student stipend was more than generous. Monica had made a couple of quips about me not having any school spirit, but mostly I could ignore her. It was amazing how easy it was to avoid someone who lived in the same suite and had most of the same classes.

I ran a hand through my hair and headed out into the common room.

"Surprise!" Terrin yelled, shoving a cupcake with a lit candle in my face.

"Shit," I exclaimed, lashing out with my arm and knocking the cupcake to the floor.

He grabbed the candle, pinching out the tiny flame, then he looked at me with sad puppy dog eyes. "I'm sorry. I only meant to surprise you for your birthday."

"How did you know?" I demanded, my hands settling on my hips.

"I asked the Headmaster," he said sheepishly.

"How did she know?"

"Mr. Reed, I think." He shrugged. "I didn't mean to scare you."

"Well you fucking did," I said and turned back toward my bedroom.

"Hailey," he said softly, reaching out a hand toward me.

"Go away, Terrin." I closed the door behind me and leaned against it. The headmaster knew when my birthday was. It was just a day, really. One's first shift happened sometime after the birthday, but everyone grew at different rates, like puberty, and it rarely happened right away. I'd been pretending it wasn't coming. That I could just hang out at Thornbriar forever. I had comfortable clothes, great food, and friends. As Terrin has said that first night, it wasn't such a bad place.

A knock came at the door. "Hailey," Terrin pleaded.

"Go away."

"Can I just talk to you please?" he asked.

"Fine," I said, letting him in. I dropped down on the end of my bed and glared at him.

"I'm sorry."

"You said that."

He rubbed a hand along the scar on his arm. "I was only trying to do something nice for my girlfriend on her birthday. Most girls would love a cupcake."

I gaped at him. There were so many things wrong with that statement, I didn't even know where to begin. "Terrin, I like you. We have fun hanging out. But you don't know me at all."

"Hailey—"

"I'm not your girlfriend."

This time, he looked surprised.

"We've never talked about it at all. You can't just decide things in your own head. A relationship is a partnership." I sighed. I sounded like one of the warden's romance book heroines, but, dammit, they were right.

"But—"

"And I'm not most girls."

"I know, Hailey. I just wanted to celebrate your birthday."

"Well, I didn't."

His mouth dropped open.

I wanted to tell him everything about my shitty life. About how birthdays weren't a great thing to be celebrated, and how I especially didn't want to celebrate this one. Because I was a spirit shifter and this was a sign of my coming doom. I stopped my speeding thoughts right there. I couldn't put that on Terrin. He was a good guy, and he didn't deserve it. I sighed. "Just go."

He started to speak, but then he stopped. "Let me know when you're ready to talk," he said quietly and left.

I gazed at the closed door. I hadn't even been awake for ten minutes and this day couldn't have gone more wrong. I was eighteen and I was doomed.

* * *

I had spoken too soon. I walked into Shifter Biology and Brenton was already glaring at me. Couldn't we be done with this damn project already?

"What's got your panties in a twist?" he sneered.

Batting my lashes at him, I said, "You, you handsome devil."

He glared at me and turned back to our microscope.

I sighed. How was I supposed to handle classwork when I needed to plan my escape? I'd been searching through the records in the library, and I still hadn't found anything about get away routes that wouldn't take me over the fence or through the gate. Part of me wished my shift would come and I could turn into a bird, then I could fly off. I frowned. But after my shift, would I be restricted to the creature of my current phase? Or would I have the option to turn into any? Or would I have to shift into all of them, before I gained control? I bit my lip. And when would the madness start? I needed to be as far away from civilization as I could get when that happened.

"Look at this," Brenton growled, backing away from the microscope. I didn't think he knew how to speak in anything but growls or sneers.

Leaning closer, I peered into it. The cells merged on the card, and I grinned. "That's it!"

"I think so," he said, inching farther away.

I blinked at him. "What, do you think I have cooties or something?"

"Leave me alone, Rosie Posie," he muttered.

"Why?" I stepped closer to him. "What's going to happen if we touch? You won't be able to control yourself?"

He snarled. "Back off."

Reaching up, I stroked his cheek with the back of my hand.

Flames erupted in his eyes and he shoved me away. I flew back toward our table, knocking the microscope over.

"What the hell?" I exclaimed.

Brenton loomed over me, his hands balled into fists. Raising one hand, he growled, "You fucking bitch."

Fear danced along my nerve endings, and I raised my hands. Was he going to punch me? For touching him? What was his problem? I yanked my hands down and glared at him. "Do your worst, Brenton."

He stood frozen, staring at me. Then with a growl, his fists came down on our table, shattering all the glass slides. The broken pieces rained over me, and I lifted my arms to protect myself. Glass sliced small cuts in my forearms, and I winced. I cried, but I wasn't really hurt.

"Brenton and Hailey!" Professor Alexander roared next to us. "What is going on here?"

Lowering my arms, I sniffed back my tears and got to my feet. I forced my voice not to tremble and said, "He pushed me."

"She ruined our experiment, sir," Brenton said. His voice was as calm and placid as a lake.

"Both of you—" The Professor pointed toward the door. "Get out of my class."

"But—" I began. Brenton was already gathering his things. He didn't care.

The Professor was turning back toward the rest of the class. "And you both receive zeros for this assignment."

"Yes, sir," Brenton said.

"That's not fair," I protested.

"It's perfectly fair, young lady." Professor Alexander shoved his finger into my chest. His brown eyes flamed. "You provoked a fire shifter."

Dammit. The Professor was a fire shifter. Of course he took Brenton's side. I exhaled. What did I care? I was getting out of Thornbriar as soon as I could anyway. I didn't need to pass the damn class. "Yes, Professor."

26

Hailey

I stomped down the steps toward the caverns for my late night swim with Adrian. My water phase continued, and I needed to keep the element satiated. The halls were silent as I headed down stairs. Dark shadows slipped over the walls from the flickering lights. They'd wired the caverns as Adrian had said, but the current appeared uneven because the light wasn't steady.

When I entered the one we'd used before, Adrian dived through the water, his pale form gleaming under the lights. As soon as he came up for breath, I said, "Adrian."

"Hey, Hailey." He waved an arm. "Come on in."

I slid off my clothes and dove into the warm water. The temperature was perfect. Warm and salty, the water unwound every tight muscle I had. I lay on my back, floating as Adrian had taught me, and tried to relax.

Trapped. I was trapped by Terrin, trapped by the school, trapped by my own powers, whatever they were. A knot settled in the pit of my stomach, and all the warm water in the world couldn't make it unwind.

Every time I floated close to Adrian, he slipped further away. What was wrong with him? I purposely floated toward him a few times, and it kept reoccurring. What was going on? Grasping the edge when I got near to it, I flipped myself upright and turned to look at him. "What's up with you?"

He looked away from me. "All good."

The knot in my gut tightened. All this shit today, and now my friend was avoiding me. "I had a fight with Terrin this morning."

"Yeah, I know."

"Did he say something to you?" I pushed off from the wall and doggie-paddled over to him.

"He cares about you, Hailey," Adrian said.

"Funny way of showing it." I grimaced. Calling me his girlfriend when he hadn't even asked and I didn't even know if I'd say yes. Now he'd obviously told his friend to back off. "I'm not his property, you know."

"What?" he asked, a frown creasing his handsome face.

"We aren't anything," I said, thinking about the pink frosting smeared floor. "Even if we had been, we basically broke up this morning."

Adrian gave a half-smile. "But you're his."

"I'm my own person."

"Of course you are," he said. "But my pack brother has an interest in you, and I'm not a poacher."

Frustration welled up in me. Terrin and I had kissed. We'd held hands. Hell, he hadn't even wanted to make love. None of it meant he owned me. He hadn't paid for me at a virgin auction. I was my own person, and I was tired of people treating me like I was bought and paid for.

Chewing on my lip, I stared at the lights along the edge of the pool. I didn't even know how much longer I'd be at Thornbriar. I was eighteen now. I could shift at any time, and then they'd all know my secret. How much longer would I even be alive after that? This was my fucking life and I wanted to make the most of it. I stared at the blond Adonis in front of me.

I reached out and grasped Adrian's shoulders. I think I caught him off guard because he let me pull his body closer. Then I pressed my lips onto his. At first, he resisted, his body stiff and unyielding against mine.

But slowly, his firm lips softened as I kissed him, parting and letting my tongue dive inside. I wrapped my arms around his neck, pressing my naked body against his. His arms came around me too, stroking my lower back. I shuddered at the jolts his touch sent through me and kissed him more deeply.

A girlish gasp echoed through the cavern, and Adrian and I jerked apart. We stared up at the brunette at the pool side, hands on her hips.

Monica said, "I knew it," and then turned on her heel and flounced off.

"I can't do this," Adrian said, shoving me away. He climbed out of the pool and grabbed his clothes.

I shivered. The pool felt cooler around me.

27

Terrin

The door shuddered with the hammering knocks. I yawned scratching my jaw as I crossed the suite. "I'm coming," I called.

I opened the door and stared at the furious brunette. "It's late, Monica."

"I caught them," she sputtered.

Rubbing my forehead, I asked, "Caught who?"

"Adrian and Hailey. Naked in the pools," she seethed. "And kissing."

"What?" I scrunched my face, trying to chase away my sleepiness.

Monica grabbed my arm. "Kissing, Terrin. They were kissing."

"Adrian and Hailey." My body tensed as I gazed at her.

"Yes."

A roar grew inside my chest, swelling up my throat. My girl. My pack mate and my girl. I grabbed a shirt off the back of the couch and slid it on. "Where?"

She led me to the stairs down to the underground caverns.

Adrian walked toward us, his head hanging. When he caught sight of me on the warpath, he raised his hands. "It wasn't what you think—"

I charged across the hall and slammed my fist into his face. His nose broke with a satisfying crunch, and he landed on his back on the floor. Blood streamed from his nostrils.

"Terrin!" Hailey cried from the stairs, and she ran across the hall. Kneeling by Adrian, she cradled him in her arms. "What is wrong with you?"

"What is wrong with me?" I growled. "You're my girl. My mate."

Hailey glared up at me. "I am not owned by you."

"Shit, Hailey. I thought you cared about me."

"I do," she said softly. "But we aren't together."

"Yes, we fucking are," I said.

She sighed. "We are dating, but we haven't had a single conversation about our relationship. I told you this morning."

I roared. The sound that came from my throat was more jungle cat than man. The hall lights swayed on their strings.

"I won't be trapped by you," Hailey said. "I won't be trapped by anyone."

"And you kissed my man," Monica shouted from behind me.

Adrian pushed up on one arm. "I'm not your fucking man, Monica. We are not dating."

We all stared at one another menacingly. Then, Monica turned and pranced away.

Hailey helped Adrian to his feet, and he held his shirt against his nose. "Let's get you to the infirmary," she said.

"And you, man. You're supposed to be my pack brother. You're supposed to have my back."

"Terrin, it didn't mean . . ." His shoulders slumped. "I didn't mean to hurt you."

He let Hailey lead him away. I just stood there, like an idiot, my fists clenching and unclenching over and over again. I'd given her my heart, and she'd betrayed me. Worse. She was an innocent and I hadn't been able to protect her from my pack mate's charm. I had failed again.

"I don't want to see either of you." I growled. "Ever again."

Hailey glanced back at me from the corner. Her chin lifted. "Don't worry. You won't."

28

Hailey

An older nurse greeted us at the door of the infirmary. She nodded her graying head. "Ah, the boys have been playing again I see."

"Playing?" I asked.

"No worries," she said. "Young shifters can get a bit rambunctious."

So, when I punched Monica, I was losing control? But when the guys hit each other, it was being rambunctious? What kind of crazy rules did this place have?

Adrian patted my arm as if he could see the annoyance on my face, and I coughed up a smile. He climbed onto the bed the nurse indicated.

She held a gauze to the bottom of his nose to staunch the blood flow, and with her other hand, she grasped mine and shoved it against the dressing. "Hold here, dear."

"Okay."

She gently washed Adrian's face. The nose didn't look that bad without the streaks of red, but it was definitely swollen. Handing me an ice pack, she said, "Hold this on his nose while I get the doctor."

I nodded. As soon as she was out of earshot, I said, "I'm so sorry, Adrian."

"Not your fault," Adrian said, breathing through his mouth.

"Yes, it is. I kissed you. You didn't want to."

"But Terrin shouldn't have been such a jerk." He winced.

I smiled. "That's true enough."

He tried to smile back. "I did enjoy kissing you."

"Me too." Squeezing his arm, I kissed his cheek. "And it's not like Terrin can be any more pissed at us."

He snorted and groaned.

A young female doctor came in and approached the bed. "Again Adrian? Whose girl you been kissing now?"

Adrian laughed and winced even harder. "They kiss me, Dr. Wang. You know that."

She chuckled. Looking over his chart, she nodded. "I'm going to have to reset the nose. Then you'll need to rest for at least a week. No strenuous activity." She looked pointedly at me, and I raised my hands.

"Swimming though, right?" he asked.

The doctor frowned. "Yes, but keep your head above water."

He moaned.

"The water will help you heal faster, but getting these bandages wet won't. Am I clear?"

"Yes, Doc."

"Okay." She gestured to me. "You might want to take his hand. This is going to hurt."

I frowned. "No pain reliever?"

"He's a shifter. He can handle it."

Holding Adrian's hand, I watched as the doctor placed her hands on his nose. Adrian tensed.

"Relax," she said soothingly as if she'd worked with many wild animals. Which I supposed she had.

Adrian took a deep breath and shrugged his shoulders.

She placed her hand on either side of his nose, and snapped it back into place in one quick motion.

He yowled and squeezed my hand. But then it was over.

The doctor handed me some gauze to mop up the blood. Then she packed his nose with more gauze and bandaged it. "Ice it every few hours until the swelling goes down, and get some rest."

Adrian nodded. "Thanks, doc."

She glanced at me. "Don't worry. Shifters heal fast. He'll be up to his old activities in no time."

I smiled.

Sliding off the table, Adrian raised an eyebrow. "I'm still handsome, right?"

"Of course," I said.

After I dropped Adrian off at his suite, I headed back to my own bed. There'd been no sign of Terrin, thank goodness. By the time I opened the door to my suite, it was after three in the morning. The outer room was silent and dark, and I opened the door to my room. I flicked on the light and stared at my bed. The bedding had been ripped to shreds with a knife or a claw. Long strips of sheets and blankets hung over my desk, my closet, and my floor. The pillows had been shredded and the stuffing dribbled across the floor.

On the wall over my bed, Monica—because who else would it have been—had scrawled in red lipstick, "Get out! You don't belong here."

Heat flushed through my body as I stared at the words. Blood rushed against my ears. These were my things. Well, not exactly mine, but gifted to me by the academy. What right did she have to destroy my stuff over a guy who didn't even want her? I was going to strangle her. I yanked open the door and marched across the common room to knock on her door.

I raised my hand and stared at it, my heart dropping into my stomach. It wasn't a hand; it was a scaly claw. Turning, I ran for the door, grasping the handle and yanking it open. I ran down the hall and the stairs, praying I made it in time. If they found a mermaid in the middle of the hall, I'd be doomed. Frantically, I tried to remember Professor Frank's meditations. I should be able to control the change. I took deep breaths, well, as deep as I could in a full sprint. As soon as I saw the first pool, I stripped and dived in. Gills opened in my chest, and I breathed water. My bones thinned and my legs merged into one long tail. Terrin had been right, it didn't hurt exactly, but a tingly feeling spread through my nerves, like every part was waking up.

In a way that I'd never been before, I was truly alive.

* * *

By the time I'd been able to shift back and gotten back to my dorm, I'd been too tired to clean up. I'd fallen asleep on top of my ripped sheets. Cracking an eye, I'd glanced at the clock and moaned. I was already late for Tutoring Assistance. Professor Ward was going to have my hide.

I'd shifted. Giddy laughter ran through me, followed by terror on its heels. Part of me wanted to run out into the woods and try to shift into every form. The other, saner part of me wanted to hide in bed all day claiming to be sick. What if they all took one look at me and knew? I hadn't known that Terrin had shifted but Adrian hadn't yet. But I didn't know what to look for. Maybe there was some telltale sign.

I grabbed a quick shower, seeing as I was late already. What did it matter? I ran a brush through my tangled hair and pulled on my favorite forest green tee shirt and jeans. I stared at my image in the mirror. My whole body vibrated and I felt as though I glowed, but the reflection only showed the same old Hailey.

I took a deep breath. Focus. Like Professor Frank had taught us.

Throwing on my new jacket, I opened the door and crossed the empty suite. I headed across campus for T.A. Everyone was already in their classes, so the halls were mostly empty. My chair in the library had a stack of new books and a list of assignments. I glanced toward Professor Ward's office, but his door was shut. Good. No confrontation to test my control. Was my transformation last night set off by my emotions? Or had it just been time?

I shrugged off my jacket and set to work. The sooner I got my schoolwork done, the sooner I could go back to looking for an escape route. I had been poring over blueprints and histories of the school to see if there might be a way out that wasn't immediately obvious. Professor Frank had said that the buildings were previously a monastery. Monks, as I discovered in my reading, liked secret rooms and passages. There must have been something I could use. They couldn't have boarded up every single one.

When I came back from the bathroom, I found a red index card in the book on school history I'd been looking at. I glanced up, but the few other students in the library at this time were engrossed in their studies. I flipped to the page marked and stared at the entry. It spoke of underground tunnels leading out of the school and down the mountain. A secret escape route.

I bit my lip. Someone had known I was looking and shared this with me. I stared at the red card. There was no writing on it. I sniffed it. No smell. Just an ordinary index card except for its bright color. Was this a gift? A threat? Did someone know my secret? I dropped into my seat.

Returning the books to the shelf, I cleaned up my chair and headed out to lunch. The quad was busy with students now. Terrin and Sciro sat on a bench to one side, with Greta's gang on the other. I took a breath and walked between them, head held high and looking straight ahead. Still no sign of Monica. Had she left the card for me in the library? Was she hiding out because she ripped up my sheets? Or was she simply busy with her own business for once? A knot curled in my stomach, but I kept my breathing even and held my focus.

The smell of chicken tortilla soup greeted my nose, the spices heavy in the air. I'd tasted so many different foods since I'd come to Thornbriar Academy. There was no telling what I'd be able to afford once I escaped. What kind of job could I get? Deep breath. Focus. No use worrying about it now. First, I had to get out, then I'd worry about where and how I'd live and eat.

I frowned. Had the guys taken Adrian some food? I guessed Terrin wouldn't, but would Sciro? Or was he having to scrounge whatever chips and soda they had laying around? I grabbed a tray and loaded it with two bowls of soup, rolls, and salad. I dropped two pieces of flan on it as well. Terrin was probably loving this meal that would remind him of home. Ducking out the back door of the dining hall, I headed toward the boys' dorm.

Hesitating at the door, I wondered if Adrian was sleeping. I knocked anyway.

"Hailey," he said with a sleepy smile. His swelling had gone down, so the white bandage perched precariously over his nose.

"I brought soup."

"Fantastic." He gestured for me to come in.

I carried the dishes to the coffee table which for once was almost clear. Adrian sank down on to the couch next to me. "What a spread."

With a shrug, I said, "I figured if I was going to bring you lunch, I should do it right."

He grinned. "Abso-fucking-lutely."

"I'm sorry." I gestured to his face. "About all this."

"You didn't hit me."

"No, but I kissed you and started it all."

He reached out and wrapped his fingers around mine. "I never regret kissing a gorgeous girl."

My cheeks felt warm. Damn blushes. "Good."

Leaning forward, he brushed his lips against mine. Warmth uncurled in my gut, loosening the knot that had been there all day. Grasping his tee shirt in my hand, I held him close and gazed into his sea-green eyes. I kissed him, and he inched closer on the sofa. My lips parted as the kiss deepened. His hand slipped across my stomach, igniting every nerve he passed.

He trailed kisses down my neck and across my chest, pushing my coat off my shoulders. I watched him hungrily.

Adrian lifted his head and met my gaze. "Hailey, is this what you want?"

"Yes," I breathed. "But what about pregnancy?"

He smiled. "Shifter biology is different than humans. There's no chance of that until we're older."

"Oh." I licked my lips. "Okay then."

His gaze heated. "Then let's adjourn to the bedroom."

I nodded.

He took my hand, pulling me to my feet, and we crossed to his bedroom. Art hung on the walls, some of naked women, but also of beaches and oceans teeming with life. I gazed around, rapt, but he tugged me toward the double bed. The sheets were black silk, soft as butter, and slid over my skin as I lay on them.

Shedding his shirt, Adrian climbed in beside me and kissed me tenderly. He slid off my tee shirt, revealing my new bra. When I'd had the choice, I'd chosen a lacy push-up one that showed my assets instead of the school-issued one. He cupped and stroked my breasts, sliding his thumb under the lace and caressing each nipple. Sensation flooded through me, and I groaned.

Reaching out, I ran my hands over the smooth skin of his chest. His muscles tightened under my touch.

He grabbed my hands and held them above my head with one hand of his. "Tsk tsk," he said. "It's not your turn yet."

I never wanted to be trapped, but this wasn't imprisonment. This was the gentle insistence that I take my pleasure first. My heart skittered against my ribs.

After dispensing, one-handed, with my bra, he put his mouth on my breasts. Passion surged through me, and I arched against him, wanting more.

"Impatient," he said, shaking his head. His practiced hand undid the fastening on my jeans.

I licked my lips, wetness flooding my panties in anticipation.

He slid his fingers into my folds, stroking my sensitive nub. I moaned. Adrian pushed two fingers inside as his thumb continued to rub circles over my core. My hips bucked. His green eyes darkened as he watched me.

My breath sped up as he drove me toward the cliff. Waves crashed over me, drowning me in pleasure. I gasped as his ministrations increased. I came, shattering and shuddering against the sea wall.

Releasing my arms, he lay down next to me, eyes smoldering. "I've wanted to do that since you punched Monica in the courtyard."

Tears welled at my eyelids. To be wanted, not just sexually, but desired for the joy of giving me pleasure. I leaned against him, catching my breath and breathing in his salty smell. "You really are amazing."

Pushing up on his elbow, he grinned down at me and winked.

I laughed.

His eyes trailed down my skin, and my laughter cut off. He stood and stripped. My mouth watered at the beautiful man that was revealed. He tugged on my jeans and underwear, sliding them down my legs and tossing them away. Spreading my legs, he slid between them. The hard length of him pressing against me made me melt.

He kissed me on the lips, softly and gently. His fingers trailed against my skin, reigniting the flames. His cock pressed against my entrance. Lifting my chin, he gazed into my eyes. "What do you want, Hailey?"

"You," I gasped.

With a smile, he pushed himself inside me, one slow inch at a time. A twinge of pain echoed in my awareness, and Adrian tensed slightly, his gaze deepening, but it was gone in an instant. My body opened to receive him, and he began to move. Ecstasy washed through me, intensifying with each thrust that came. We fell into a natural rhythm, meeting each other at the central point. I moaned as the pace increased and we approached the pinnacle together. When it hit, we clung to each other shuddering.

29

Adrian

Hailey and I eventually made it out to our cold lunch, but it was amazing anyway. I hadn't wanted to say goodbye, but she'd insisted that she'd missed enough classes and I needed to rest. I didn't know about that. I felt amazing. I almost hated to wash away her scent with a shower, but I needed one.

Stripping again, I headed into the spray. I scrubbed down, remembering the feel of her hands on my skin, and turned the dial a little colder. Pausing my soaping, I scratched my shoulder, wondering if I'd gotten a bug bite there. I shrugged. The light in her eyes when I'd brought her pleasure made me groan. I scrubbed my skin harder. Lingering under the water, I knew I needed to get down to the pools even if my nose wasn't ready yet. My shifter side wanted to be immersed in water. A shower wouldn't satisfy him for long.

When I couldn't put it off any more, I flipped off the shower and grabbed my towel. As I dried off, I glanced in the mirror and froze. Outlined across the top of my shoulder was the dark lines of a new tattoo. Adrian the Casanova of Thornbriar Academy had been marked.

"No, no," I muttered, scraping the vines with my towel. They didn't budge. "Shit."

How had this one girl done this to me? I liked Hailey. I'd enjoyed our time together, but I wasn't ready to make this kind of commitment. Despite their fight, part of me still believed she was Terrin's. This was just the start of the tattoo. If we never touched again, would it fade? I'd never heard of a mate mark doing that.

"Hey, Adrian," Sciro shouted from the main room, then his voice trailed off.

Shit.

Sciro had a vampire's heightened senses. He'd smell what we'd done, and he'd know who I'd done it with. I wrapped my towel around my hips and tossed another one over my shoulders. I stepped out into the main room. "Hey, Sciro."

He arched an accusing eyebrow. "She's Terrin's."

"He has nothing to do with this," I said.

Rubbing his head, Sciro sighed. "It was consensual."

"Of course it was fucking consensual," I snarled. "What do you take me for?"

"You knew she was a virgin?"

Nodding, I glared at him. "How do you know?"

"The blood." He grimaced. "Terrin broke your nose for kissing her. What do you think he's going to do to you now?"

"He said he never wanted to see either of us again."

Sciro's shoulders slumped. "He'd have forgiven y'all eventually."

"Would he?" Closing my eyes, I took a breath and then stalked toward my bedroom.

"Adrian?"

I stopped, facing my door. "Yes?"

"Was it worth it?" His voice had an odd quality to it, almost wistfulness.

Terrin. The mate bond. The look in Hailey's eyes when I made her come. "Completely."

He exhaled, and I marched into my bedroom.

30

Hailey

I kept finding myself staring out the window and brushing my fingers across my lips the rest of the afternoon. I knew I should have been concentrating on what the teachers were saying or on my escape plans, but all I could think about was Adrian's lips on mine.

When Professor Roth dismissed the class, I gathered my books and turned to leave.

"Hailey." Brenton glared at me.

Well, that was a cold shower. I sighed. "Yeah?"

"Why weren't you in Bio today?"

I snorted. "None of your business."

"You already caused me to get a zero," he growled.

"Yes," I said, glancing across the classroom to Terrin. I tried to catch his eye, but he ignored me just as he said he would. I knew I should give him his space, but I didn't want to leave without saying goodbye.

Turning to Brenton, I said, "And you should be glad that we're not partnered anymore. The project's over."

Brenton's eyes narrowed. "Professor Alexander decided it would be good practice for my control if we remained partners."

"What?" I whipped around and stared at Brenton.

He gave an exaggerated sigh. "I said, he's my fire shifter mentor and he thinks that . . ."

"I don't care what he thinks." I frowned. "And why do you have a mentor? Is that a thing?"

He growled. "It's T.A. for focus. They think I fly off the handle too . . ."

I raised an eyebrow, and he stopped.

"Never mind. We're partners until the end of term," he muttered and stomped off.

Taking a deep breath, I reminded myself that I was leaving. I just had to figure out how. Rustling through my pack, I pulled out the notes I'd made about the tunnel. I should go and check it out.

I headed down the stairs toward the pools, hearing the laughing and splashing of other water shifters. With a frown, I retreated back upstairs. I wasn't going to be able to explore when they were all down there. Tonight, I'd head down. Maybe I'd see Adrian again and we could . . . heat rose in my cheeks at the thought.

Later that night, the rare warm evening meant the courtyard was packed. I saw Adrian's blond head bent in conversation. I grinned and strode over.

He stood and looked down at Monica.

I stopped, frowning. He was probably telling her off for turning us in to Terrin.

Adrian brushed her curls out of her eyes and smiled down at her.

He was flirting? My mer-creature screamed inside of me, the wail echoing against my temples. I blinked at the unusual pain.

I shook myself. No, we'd had sex, but Adrian and I hadn't made any commitments. He'd been tender and kind, everything I'd hoped for my first time. I liked him, and while it could grow into something more, I didn't have the right to ask it of him. I knew he was a womanizer. I'd known it before we made love. Besides, I was leaving soon, and likely we'd never see each other again.

My mer-creature cried out again in anguish. I could almost picture her tearing at her long green locks. It had to be something to do with being a shifter. Had there been a mate's mark? I shoved up my sleeve and stared at my shoulder. There was nothing there. If we hadn't marked, why was my creature pissed?

I frowned at Adrian and looked back at my shoulder, but nothing had changed.

A growl echoed behind me, and I swung around.

"You fucked him?" Terrin said, anger flowing off him in waves. It seemed to heat the air around me, and goose-bumps broke out across my skin.

My jaw fell open. "How did you know?"

"You were looking for a mate mark," he muttered. Turning away, his broad shoulders hunched.

I swallowed. "There isn't one."

He ignored me and strode toward the building. I closed my eyes. He'd left me again and it hurt in ways I hadn't expected.

I glanced back toward Adrian, but he hadn't even looked up. I cared about both of them, and they'd both given up on me.

Wrapping my arms around myself, I turned back toward the dorms. It was a good thing, sort of. I could run, disappear through the tunnels and no one would even notice I was gone. It was for the best.

My heart ached as I slowly climbed the stairs. Best to go tonight, before it got any worse. There was no one and nothing for me here. The suite was empty. Everyone really was at dinner. I grabbed a bag, and packed a few clothes, and some snacks the guys had shown me how to order. Then, I looked around, but there was nothing else. A few books, mostly from the library and the school uniforms. Not likely to need those outside, and I wouldn't want anything to lead back here.

I shut the door with a sigh. My mer-creature still whined within me, but I ignored her. My chest felt hollow, echoing with each beat of my heart. I crossed toward the hall with the library and the stairwell down to the pools.

"Planning a heist, Rosie?" a deep voice inquired.

With a groan, I glanced up at the dark shape approaching me. "What do you want, Brenton?"

He didn't answer, just stated, "You weren't at the party."

"Is that what that was?"

"The loathsome ones seemed to think so." He quirked an eyebrow.

Ignoring his overture, I kept walking toward the stairs. "Go bother someone else. I have places to be."

He reached out a hand and grasped my arm. "And where would that be?"

His hand. On my arm. It had to be the first time Brenton had ever intentionally touched me. Why now? Of all times? "I'm going for a swim."

"What have you got in there? Diving equipment? The pools aren't that deep."

I glared at him. "None of your business."

He looked down, scuffing his feet on the rough floor.

Shrugging off his hand, I muttered, "Go away, Brenton," and headed down the stairs. At least he didn't follow me.

My footsteps echoed in the silent pools. No one swam tonight. The lights flickered on and off. The smell of the saltwater hit my nose, and I sniffed. Adrian hadn't made any promises to me. I hadn't made any to him, either. That's what I wanted. I called the shots. We made love, but he didn't owe me anything. I'd known I was going to leave.

Isn't that why I'd broken up with Terrin? If we'd even really been together. He wanted to make all the decisions for me. All the choices.

Running my hand along the slick rock walls, I followed the pools back through several caverns until there were only caves. The lighting stopped, and I pulled a flashlight from my bag. I'd borrowed it from the science lab, along with some extra batteries. I didn't know how deep I was going to have to go in order to find the way out.

I was a spirit shifter. They were all in danger the longer they knew me. Either the Council would execute me, or I'd go crazy and have to be put down. Or worse, I'd kill everyone. I needed to leave. It was better this way.

31

Terrin

Heading back up to the suite, I tried to choke down some chips, but I wasn't hungry. I'd cared about her so much, I'd been willing to wait until she was ready. Yet, she'd gone and had sex with Adrian. I wanted to be angry with her, but mostly I was pissed at myself.

I knew Adrian was a ladies' man. He'd had sex with nearly every girl he ever encountered. But I had trusted him, as a pack mate, to leave Hailey alone. I'd been wrong, so fucking wrong.

Squeezing my hands into fists, I slammed them down onto the glass coffee table. It shattered, and I stared at my hands, bloody and broken. She'd been a virgin. Something precious and untouched. Someone that needed protection, and I'd introduced her to the wolf. How could I have been such an idiot?

Suddenly the room felt too small, my skin too tight. I slammed open the door and headed down the stairs to the back yard. I was half-way across the yard when I realized I had already shifted, my clothes left behind me in shreds. The cat leapt into the woods, running. We dived over roots and around bushes and forded streams. We ran until we hit the property line, nearly slamming into the iron fence. The electric loops on top glinted in the moonlight.

I'd met Hailey at the fence, the section closer to campus, that first night. She'd told me she wanted to be free. Sciro said it was because of her past, but I'd never even asked. I didn't want to know about the time before I could protect her, all the hurt she'd experienced that I couldn't control.

My jaguar huffed. Then I'd caused her more pain. I'd wanted to keep her safe. I shivered in the cool night air and realized I'd returned to human form, laying naked against the fence.

I never cried. Even when I'd returned home from my last mission to find my grandmother, my aunts and uncles all lying in pools of their own blood. The drug cartel I'd been hunting had murdered everyone I'd ever cared about. I'd stood stiff and silent as the police came and cleaned up the mess. Mr. Reed had led me away, telling me about a magical place called Thornbriar Academy, where I'd be protected.

I hadn't told him I could protect myself. Though I could. I just couldn't protect those I loved.

32

Hailey

The tunnels went on forever. I tried to remember what the book had said, but it seemed a long time ago when I'd found the red card. Every time the tunnel split, I took the right path, hoping it would lead me out. They had to go somewhere right? I sighed. I just hoped I wasn't being led around in circles.

Even assuming I did get out, where was I going to go? I had thought to the beach. Although what would I really find there? I didn't know much about my real family. I'd been so young when I was taken, only seven. Forcing my mind to think back, I tried to dredge up some memories. A homemade birthday cake with a lopsided "H" in happy. The beach, building sandcastles and playing in the waves. Crunching sand between my toes.

Hailey Cooper. I had lied to the Headmaster. I did remember my last name, but I didn't see how it would do her any good. Nothing distinctive about it at all. There must be a million families with the name Cooper. It seemed like a small thing to hold back, but I had so few things that belonged to me. Giving up the name would have been like giving up a part of myself.

A dark shape darted by my feet, and my flashlight bounced wildly. "A rat, a rat," I reassured myself. I shivered in the cool dampness of the caves. The heat of the day didn't reach down here. Pausing, I rummaged in my bag for my jacket and pulled it on. See, like a girl scout, Hailey Cooper was prepared for everything. And boy did it feel weird to call myself by my full name, even in my head.

The silence of the evening stretched before me, and I realized how much I'd gotten used to the sounds of other students going about the dorm or even the other girls at Hastings House. I hadn't been alone very often in my life, other than times I'd been punished in the closet.

I was going to miss Thornbriar. A lump formed in my throat. I'd miss the easy companionship of Terrin and Adrian and Sciro. Well, before they'd turned on me. I'd miss being around people who understood how my skin itched when I needed to change. How a plate of food could turn me into a ravenous beast. I smiled. The guys had all laughed at how much I ate and how much I enjoyed my food.

Rubbing my stomach, I wished I'd brought more than a few breakfast bars. Who knew how long this trip was going to be? And I was already hungry.

Water dripped up ahead, and I hurried forward to see if there was a stream or something I could follow. I flashed my light along the wall, but there were only rivulets of water running down the stone. Something above ground was dripping inside. Had it started raining? Or was there a creek above me? No telling.

I shook my head and continued on. It was going to be lonesome out in the world without the guys. Who would I run in the woods with? Who would go swimming with me? Who would watch bad movies and eat popcorn? I grimaced. I'd be fine. I just had to learn to be happy alone. Thinking about all those spirit shifters in the books, I figured I probably shouldn't live too close to civilization anyway. I was dangerous.

The guys were better off without me. Adrian had moved on, and Terrin would find some other girl to protect. Who knew when I'd go crazy?

What if I'd attacked them? It was better this way.

I kicked a rock across the floor. Would these tunnels ever end? I couldn't see more than a few feet ahead of me or behind me, only what was visible in my flashlight's beam. Was there more than rats in here? Suddenly, I wished I'd brought more than clothes and a little food. What if I needed a weapon? I didn't think shifting into a mermaid in a dry cave would help.

Sciro had said I'd be able to shift into anything, but I still didn't know if I was limited by my phase or if I could change into anything at any time. I stopped and set down my bag. Closing my eyes, I imagined running after rabbits and howling at the moon. I tried to see myself as the wolf. The images ran through my mind's eye, but my body stayed human. Was I not focused enough? Professor Frank would have said so. My lips quirked. She always said I didn't have enough focus. I needed to practice more.

I glanced back at the dark tunnel. Was I throwing away my only chance to learn how to be what I was? I didn't even know where I was going. Would I wander around these caves forever, getting more and more lost? Would I die in here? I grabbed my bag and ran forward. There had to be an end to these tunnels somewhere.

33

Terrin

"So, that's how it's going to be, is it?" Sciro's voice cut through the fog of pain.

Glaring at him, I muttered, "Go away, brother."

He snorted. "What kind of brother would I be if I left you out here by yourself?" He held up a cotton school robe. "You want this? Or you gonna shift back so we can go for a proper run?"

"I'll take the robe," I said, standing.

"Good." He searched my face. "You found out, didn't you?"

I frowned. "How'd you know?"

"Blood," he growled. "And she smells like a fucking flower."

"Lavender."

He grunted.

I yanked on the robe, and we started back through the woods. "I should have listened to you."

"What do you mean?"

"You said I should talk to her." I hunched my shoulders.

"Communication is the key, man," he said, sounding like some talk-show guru.

I laughed harshly. "Where'd you read that?"

"Street smarts, man." He raised a cocky eyebrow, then he frowned. "It's not your job to protect her, you know."

"Good thing, cause I fucking suck at it."

Sciro stopped. "No. That's not what I meant."

I eyed him, my cat eyes nearly as good as his vampire ones in the gathering darkness.

"I meant, Hailey's strong. She's had to be, growing up where she did."

"Yeah," I said. "She doesn't need me."

"She does, but not in the way you think. She doesn't need protection, but she does need a friend, someone to listen and be there for her."

"I tried to be her friend."

"She needs someone to give her," he continued, "what she's been missing for so long: love."

"I love her." As I said the words, I realized they were true.

"That's what she needs, man. Unconditional love."

I grimaced. "But she doesn't love me. She slept with Adrian."

"After you pushed her away." Sciro huffed. "I'm just saying, man, that you have to understand where she's coming from. Hailey has been held hostage her whole life. She just wants to be free."

"And what, I'm smothering her?"

Sciro raised that damn eyebrow again. "Might be worth thinking about."

We came out of the woods and headed up the lawn toward the dorm. A dark shape ran toward us, huffing, and we both peered at Brenton the asshole uneasily.

"Where the hell have you been?" he asked.

"None of your business."

He sneered. "Your girl's all packed up to run away. Thought you'd want to know."

"What?" I grabbed the front of his shirt, twisting it in my hand. "What did you do to her?"

Raising his fist, he growled, "Get your hands off me, Matos."

Sciro grabbed my arm. "Let him go, Terrin."

I relaxed my grip and said, "Tell me."

Brenton was furious, but he held himself in check. I would have been pretty impressed, actually, if he hadn't been talking about Hailey.

"Saw her headed down into the caverns with a full bag," he said. "Way more than a swimsuit and a towel. More like her entire wardrobe."

A frown crossed my face. "Meeting Adrian?"

"No. He was still in the courtyard flirting with that Monica chick, when I came out here." Brenton met my gaze directly. "She's running away."

My skin prickled. "But there's thousands of caves down there. She'll get lost."

"Someone must have told her there's a way out." Brenton said.

"Oh, shit," Sciro said. "And all Hailey wants is to be free."

I turned and started running toward the buildings.

"Wait, Terrin," Sciro said. "We need Adrian. He knows those caves better than any of us."

"Then get him. I'll meet you down there."

Sciro nodded and took off toward the courtyard.

It wasn't until I was halfway down the stairs to the caverns that I realized Brenton was still on my heels. I swung around. "Why are you following me?"

He froze. "I just thought I'd help."

"Well, I don't want your help." I took a breath, trying to focus. My thoughts were racing with what danger Hailey might be in. What if we never found her?

I said, "Look man. You brought me the info. I appreciate it. I do." I sighed. "But we'll take it from here."

Brenton shrugged. "More bodies means more help. But if you don't want me, I'll go."

"You should do that." I watched him lumber up the steps for a minute, and then I continued down-stairs. I stared at the flickering lights. There were so many caves and tunnels leading away from the pools. How were we going to find her? I frowned. We had to. I wouldn't fail Hailey again.

34

Adrian

My shoulder itched and I was getting cold. I'd lingered in the courtyard with Monica, not wanting to run into Hailey or go back to the dorm and encounter Terrin. The confrontation with Sciro had been enough for one day. I knew I was in denial, but I wasn't ready to be mated. I had more life to live, dammit.

I grimaced, glancing at Monica. I wasn't being fair to her, though. I knew she liked me, and I was using her to avoid another chick. I was an asshole.

Sciro came pelting across the yard, full vampire speed.

Shoving down my jealousy, I raised an eyebrow at him. "What's the emergency?"

"Hailey's running away."

"What?" I straightened, feeling Monica stiffen on the seat next to me. She didn't turn around and pretended to ignore Sciro, but her body language betrayed her.

"She thinks there's some escape route through the caverns."

I jumped to my feet. "But there's miles of tunnels. She could be lost for weeks."

Sciro nodded. "Come on, man. We got to meet Terrin down there. No one knows the caves like you do."

"I don't understand. How would she have even gotten the idea?" Then it hit me, and I rounded on her. "Monica," I growled.

She batted her eyelashes at me. "What, Adrian-honey?"

I wasn't fooled for a second. Monica was an open book to me. "What did you tell Hailey about the caves?"

"Nothing," she said sweetly.

Fury roared through me like I'd never felt before. I grabbed Monica and yanked her up to face me. "What did you do?"

She trembled under my hands. Her gaze darted around me, looking for someone to help, but no one stepped forward.

I leaned closer, laying my face alongside her head. "Tell me."

"I just wanted her to go away," she said. "To leave us alone."

My gaze held the full weight of my anger, and Monica flinched. She knew me, too, even if she sometimes chose to ignore what I told her.

"So it could be the way it was before," she whined.

"Monica," I growled.

"I left that book out. The one you showed me about how the monks used the old tunnels to smuggle slaves off the mountain."

I stared at her. Those tunnels had been closed down for years. Some had caved in, and others were in danger of collapsing too. And she'd sent my mate down there. I didn't even know what I was doing, but I started to shake Monica until her teeth rattled.

Sciro grabbed my arm. "Adrian. We don't have time for this. We need to go."

I took a breath and nodded. Releasing her, I turned away.

"Adrian," Monica pleaded.

Sciro and I took off for the caverns, and I left my oldest friend behind.

We hit the stairs running, and I dredged up every fact I'd learned about the caverns over the years. I'd been fascinated by them when I'd first arrived at Thornbriar. The pools were a fairly recent addition, added when the shifters turned the old monastery into a school.

Terrin had already charged into the caves, not thinking that now we'd have two people to look for, not just one.

Sciro turned to me. "How do we do this? It won't do us any good to get lost too."

"We need cable and something to hold it here." I pointed to the edge of the pool, where a ladder protruded. "Then we can follow the cable back."

"Okay, let's go get supplies," Sciro said, turning.

"I've got them," Brenton said behind us, dropping rope and fastenings to the ground. Over his shoulders, he had two or three bulging gym bags, and the big guy was barely breaking a sweat.

Sciro and I both stared at him. "Why are you here?"

"Can't lose my lab partner." He shrugged.

I blinked. *What the hell?* But there was no doubt we needed his help. We'd rushed off to find Hailey, but hadn't even thought to bring supplies. Some friends we were.

From one of his gym bags, Brenton pulled out brightly colored chalk.

"What's that for?" Sciro asked. I could almost see his analytical mind processing.

"To mark the paths we've tried." Brenton lifted flashlights out of another bag.

I didn't know what to say to that, so I bent down and started tying ropes to the ladder.

Terrin came charging out of the caves, huffing. He stared at us all wild-eyed.

Sciro got in his face. "Stop, Terrin. We've got a plan."

If it'd have been anyone else, they'd have ended up with a broken nose to match mine. I rubbed the bandage still covering it.

We worked fast, tying the other ends of the ropes around our waists. Then we headed in, and every time the path split, we each chose a different path. We'd go as far as we could on that path, then turn around and come back. We marked each path that didn't lead anywhere.

On the first round, I found a recent cave-in, dust rising around it.

"Hailey?" I'd called but there's been no response. I started digging out the rocks, hoping she wasn't in here.

I didn't want the mate mark, but I also didn't want her to be hurt. Everything within me called out to claim and take care of her. She was ours, my creature and mine. I rubbed a dusty hand across my brow. We had to find her.

35

Sciro

I followed the tunnel, listening to the water dripping above. Pausing, I closed my eyes and smelled, using my vampiric senses to my advantage. The heavy mineral smell of the rocks almost covered it over, but the tunnel had a hint of Hailey's lavender scent. She'd come this way.

My flashlight dangled from my hand. I didn't need extra light to see in the dark. "Hailey?" I called.

We were going to find her. We had to.

The look on Terrin's face when he'd come out of the cave . . . my brother was heartbroken and determined and pissed off all at once.

Once we found her, Terrin would have to be the one to convince her to stay. If Adrian or I or even Brenton did it, Terrin would give up. He'd think she wasn't meant to be his, and that wasn't true. I'd seen them together. Terrin and Hailey made sense.

Adrian would just go on to his next conquest. Terrin truly loved Hailey. If he could just get over his dickish controlling shit, he'd be perfect for her. He cared, no matter how scared he was, and he was gentle. He'd always be there for her, supporting her no matter what. He was just what Hailey needed.

I headed toward a corner, and froze. My vampire senses picked up Hailey just beyond the next wall. She was low to the ground, probably sitting, and I heard the soft click of a water bottle being opened. Hailey sighed. She sounded tired, even though she'd only been down here a couple of hours.

I listened thoughtfully, then I turned around and headed back along my rope. I used my speed, to race back down the line, and then I picked out Terrin's rope and I tugged on it.

He came charging back down the passage. His night vision was almost as good as mine. "Where is she?"

I inclined my head toward the tunnel. "That way, just keep taking the rights and you'll find her near the sound of water."

His hands tightened into fists. "Why didn't you bring her back?"

"Terrin, listen to me," I said placidly. "She's safe. She's okay. But you need to be the one to bring her back."

He frowned as he considered what I'd said, then he nodded. "Right turns?"

I slapped him on the shoulder. "You've got this man. I'll get rid of the other guys. Bring her home."

Terrin took off down the tunnel I'd indicated. I gave him a few minutes, then I tugged on the lines of the other guys. We'd clean up the rest, and Terrin would bring our girl home.

36

Hailey

I lay against the rock, my eyes closing. It'd been a long day, and there was a long way to go. It wouldn't hurt for me to rest. I didn't even know if there was an end to these tunnels. I'd come across two cave-ins already, and I feared that I'd stumble into something I couldn't get out of.

The water still trickled above. I was starting to worry that I'd been going in circles all evening. I was never going to find a way out, and I'd given up what I'd had at Thornbriar for nothing. I'd given up Adrian and Terrin and Sciro, who had all, in their own ways, been kind to me.

Spirit shifters always went mad. My chest tightened. I couldn't bear to hurt anyone. The accounts from the books I'd read trooped through my head. I grimaced. But when had they really started killing them off? Had spirit shifters ever had the benefit of Professor Frank's focus training? If I worked really hard at focus training, could I stay in control? I couldn't imagine hurting Terrin or Adrian or even Sciro. I was so deep in my thoughts; I didn't hear his footsteps approach.

"Hailey," Terrin said gruffly.

My eyes popped open, and I stared at him. "What are you doing here?"

"I came to rescue . . . find you." He grinned, illuminating his face with his flashlight.

I bit my lip. "I'm glad you did."

"I was hoping you would be." Terrin came over and squatted down next to me. "I'm sorry, Hailey."

"Sorry for what?"

"For not protecting you," he sighed. "And I know that's not what you want to hear."

"I can take care of myself." I twisted my hands in my lap.

"I know you can. You're brave and strong and fearless."

My mouth quirked. "But . . ."

"I grew up with my grandmother in Mexico." He shifted uncomfortably, and I reached out and took his hand. He curled his fingers around mine.

"She believed that I was an ancient spirit reborn."

"A what?"

"Among our people, they tell the story of a shape-shifter who turns into a jaguar."

"Like you."

"Yeah, and the shape shifter's duty is to root out and kill murderers." He scratched at his neck. "Grandmother trained me to be a killer, and I murdered many people."

"Bad people . . ."

He shrugged. "It doesn't matter. They still died by my hand."

I waited for him to continue. He blamed himself for what his grandmother had made him do. My heart ached for him.

"Eventually, the drug cartel figured out who was killing off their best guys. They sent an assassin to my house, and they killed my grandmother, my aunts and uncles . . . even my little cousins. They left their bodies where they fell."

Squeezing his hand, I said, "You think you should have protected them."

"Shouldn't I have?" he asked, his shoulder shaking. "I was supposed to be the superhero ridding the world of villains, and I couldn't even safeguard my own family."

I wrapped my arms around him, just holding him.

"I came to Thornbriar after that." He took a breath. "And then I find you. This amazing light in all of this dark life, and I just want to hold on to you forever."

I gave a small smile. "And keep me safe."

He nodded. "Only I couldn't. Because I didn't protect you from my brother. I didn't save you from Adrian."

"Oh, Terrin." I shook my head. "I didn't need protection from Adrian."

"But—"

"I care about him, and I chose to make love to him." I squeezed his arm. "He didn't trick me or seduce me or whatever you are thinking."

He tensed. "You love him?"

"I don't know," I said honestly. "I care about both of you very much."

"Is this because of the freedom thing?" he asked, and I could tell he was thinking about the first night we'd met by the fence.

"Yes. I was held captive for most of my life." He shuddered. I studied him in the dim light. "Do you want to hear this?"

He unwound himself from my arms and turned so we sat face to face. Then he clasped both of my hands in his, and looked at me. "I do."

I told him about Hastings House and my life there. He listened as I spoke of how Mr. Hastings meant to auction off my virginity. How he had owned every part of my life except for my shifting dreams. "I need to be free in spirit as well as body. In some ways, Thornbriar has felt like just another form of captivity."

"And my clinginess even more."

I winced. "I'm sorry. I can't live like that anymore."

He rubbed his thumbs over mine. "I want you to come back, Hailey.

To Thornbriar and to me." He took a breath. "But I want you to do it on your terms. I can't promise I won't want to protect you, but I'll do my best to let you spread your wings."

Staring into his eyes, I knew that I'd never wanted anything more. I had an opportunity at Thornbriar to learn about my shifter nature that I wouldn't get anywhere else. Even if I could find a spirit shifter colony, who said they would take me in and not shoot me on sight? But also, I had someone who cared about me for the first time in my life. I didn't want to throw that away.

What if Adrian came to his senses and decided that he still wanted me? Could Terrin accept that kind of freedom? I bit my lip, staring at him. "I won't be your girlfriend."

"What do you mean?"

"I need to be free to choose," I said. "This is my first chance to experience life. Give me time to live before I settle down." I stroked the edge of his face. "But I definitely want you along for the ride. If you're willing?"

"Hailey, I love you, and I want to be with you no matter what."

I leaned forward and kissed him, pushing him back against the cavern floor. His mouth opened to me, and I nipped his lower lip.

Our kiss deepened. Straddling him, I let my hands trail over his chest. He groaned. I stared down at my conquest, feeling powerful in a way I never had before. I rocked my core against him.

"Hailey," he gasped, his hands holding me against him.

With a smile, I ripped his shirt from collar to hem. Then, I kissed and stroked his smooth muscled pecs. I'd fantasized about getting to touch him like this. He writhed beneath my careful attentions.

"Hailey," he said, his topaz eyes watching me.

I circled my hips, and he growled. His hands slid up my thighs and cupped my ass.

He squeezed and smiled when I squealed. "Do I have to rip your clothes off too?"

With a chuckle, I shucked my shirt and bra. He grabbed my shoulders and rolled me over so he was on top.

Terrin rained kisses along my throat and neck while his fingers made fast work of my jeans and panties. Everywhere his bare skin touched mine, fire erupted and I moaned.

He kissed and sucked along my torso, and I closed my eyes, sensations flooding me. He pressed his hand against my most sensitive parts. I wriggled against him, wanting more. He put his mouth to my sex, and I couldn't even breathe. When his tongue flicked over my clit, I cried out and rocked against him. Pressure built, and I writhed, grasping at his hair. I screamed his name as I exploded.

Not giving me any time to recover, he flipped me over on to my stomach and drew his hands down my back and over my ass. I shuddered, caught between wanting him to stop and to never stop.

Then, I was suddenly cold and shivery. I looked back to see where he had gone, and he stood naked and glorious behind me. At the sight of his hard rod, I licked my lips.

He smiled, a grin of pure male enjoyment. He liked that I was looking at him.

Kneeling behind me, he lifted my hips and pressed himself against my entrance. Leaning down, he brushed my hair away from my ear, and said, "Are you sure?"

"Yes."

He slid inside me, slow at first, allowing me to get accustomed to his size. His fingers stroked softly along my back and I arched, pushing back against him. He grunted.

Then, he circled his hips, and I gasped, "Terrin."

Angling himself, he drove his thrust into my pleasure spot and I cried out. His long and powerful strokes dragged me to the very edge, my breath quickening and my fingers clutching at the hard stone. Then, he'd slow, almost pause, until I moaned, "Please."

Finally, we crossed the threshold, together, bodies slick and hot. We shattered into a kaleidoscope of bliss, melting into one another.

He curled his body around me, holding me close.

37

Hailey

Terrin and I walked out of the tunnel together, my bag slung over his shoulder. We rolled up the rope, and carted it along with us.

"Brenton brought it," he said, looping it over one arm.

I laughed, then realizing he was serious, asked, "Really?"

"Yeah." He shrugged. "Said he couldn't be short a lab partner."

That only made me laugh harder. We crossed the green and had started up the stairs before I realized he was taking me to his suite. I stopped, and Terrin glanced back at me.

"Where are we going?" I asked, biting my lip.

He took my hand in his and squeezed. "I'm not willing to let go of you quite yet."

I hesitated.

"You can sleep on the couch if you want." His eyes pleaded with me. "But I need you close by tonight."

"I guess I gave you a scare."

He nodded. "Would you mind just this once?"

I exhaled. "Okay."

We continued up the stairs and down the hall to the suite. Opening the door, the sound of car crashes and whoops of joy greeted us. Adrian and Sciro were on the couch, each holding a controller in their hand. When they caught sight of us, they paused the game and gazed at us. Sciro sniffed, and a smile ghosted across his face.

Adrian scanned me from head to toe and asked, "You're okay?"

"Yes."

Terrin dropped the rope on the floor. "Hailey's staying here tonight."

"In your room?" Adrian asked softly.

"No, on the couch." He tossed my bag at Adrian. "So, time to clean up."

Sciro and Adrian hopped off the couch as if it was on fire. They cleared the wrappers and controllers and turned off the game. Their faces were serious and closed, and I rolled my eyes.

"Hey," I said. "Turn the game back on. I want to play."

"It's late," Terrin began, but then he stopped. He shrugged and gestured to the couch. "Whatever the lady wants, the lady gets."

I took a seat on the couch, and Adrian handed me a controller, his hand brushing mine. I smiled at him, and he looked away. What was going on with him? *We have sex and then he's treating me like a leper.* Then again, when we first came in, he looked genuinely concerned. We were going to have to talk soon.

Terrin sat on one side of me and Sciro on the other. Adrian perched on the arm of the sofa as if he couldn't quite pull himself away. They set about teaching me how to play the video game. I controlled a car and the goal was to crash into as many other vehicles as possible. Soon we were laughing as if I hadn't just run away, and I knew I was exactly where I needed to be.

38

Sciro

I t was two or three in the morning by the time Hailey passed out, her head on Terrin's lap and her feet on me. Adrian cleared the game controllers and the snacks out of the way and fetched an extra pillow from the closet. Terrin and I lifted her, laying her on the couch.

Adrian handed Terrin a school blanket. "Are we good, man?"

Terrin studied him for a moment, his topaz eyes glowing in the nearly dark room. "Yeah, we're good."

I let out the breath I didn't even know I'd been holding. The fracture I'd felt in our friendships had eased and our pack mates were bonded once more. All was right in the world.

Terrin bent over to drape the blanket over Hailey, and I glimpsed the leaf and vine pattern along his shoulder.

"Terrin, man, you've bonded," I said with a grin. *I knew it.*

He lifted his hand and ran it along his shoulder and then he smiled back. His cat's purr was faintly audible.

I glanced over at Adrian, to share our joy. He stood frozen in the flashing light from the screen, his face stricken. My smile fell. Something was wrong. I'd never expected Adrian to be jealous of a mate mark. "What's the matter, man?"

Terrin gazed at him too, his eyebrows drawing together. "Yeah, what's up? I thought we were good?"

Adrian yanked his tee shirt off, exposing his shoulder. I shook my head. No, that couldn't be right, could it? A green leaf and vine pattern ran over his shoulder blade.

A growl erupted from Terrin. "Whose mate are you?"

"Hailey's," Adrian said, looking down at the sleeping form on the couch.

"That's not possible," I said. "It must have been someone else. Who else have you slept with recently?"

He shook his head. "No one else for weeks."

"But it's impossible for someone to have two mates, isn't it?" Terrin turned pleading eyes to me.

I racked my brain, thinking through the loopholes. "I can only think of one other case . . ." My voice trailed off. Professor Ward's doomed romance. I closed my eyes.

Hailey had been looking at the spirit shifter books in the library. I'd told her they were dangerous, that they went mad. The fear in her eyes. No. It couldn't be, could it?

"What is it?" Terrin said.

My mouth opened and closed. I glanced back and forth between my two friends, and to the girl on the couch. Had I just doomed my brothers? I sent Terrin in. I encouraged his relationship with her.

"Don't worry." I tried to keep my voice as calm as I could, even though my stomach was sinking to my knees. "I'll research. I'm sure it's happened before."

Turning away from them, I marched into my bedroom. There had to be another explanation. Hailey couldn't be a spirit shifter. It had to be a fluke.

I sank down onto my bed, my head in my hands.

* * *

Fate had taken away Hailey's choices, mating her to two guys. Will Hailey find a way to have both freedom and love? What will happen when her deadly secret falls into the wrong hands? Find out in Bound, the second book in the Thornbriar Academy series. Grab Bound now.

ABOUT THE AUTHOR

I devoured my mother's Gothic romance collection as a teen, so dark romance and I go way back. I love sexy paranormal stories with strong heroines and gorgeous men. The only thing better than reading a good book is writing one. Thank you for coming along on Hailey's first adventures, and I hope you pick up, Bound, book two in the Thornbriar Academy series.

Say hello to Cali online:
   www.calimann.com
   www.facebook.com/groups/calispack
   www.facebook.com/calimannauthor/

ALSO BY CALI MANN

Thornbriar Academy series
Lost
Found
Bound
Saved
Bloody Lucky (a Thornbriar Academy side story)
Beautiful & Deadly (Boxset)

Misfit of Thornbriar Academy series
Infiltrate
Destroy

Shifter Island
Uncursing Her Bears
Finding Their Mermaid

Hell-Baited Wolves series
Cowritten with Freya Black
Guarded by Hellhounds
Called
Scorned
Unleashed
Charming Her Wolves (boxset)

Silver Springs Shared World
Peppermint
Cowritten with Elena Gray
Mars

Standalones:
Dark Magic